# ELIZA PROKOPOVITS

# Her Forgotten Sea

*Copyright © 2023 by Eliza Prokopovits*

*All rights reserved. No part of this publication may be reproduced, stored or transmitted in any form or by any means, electronic, mechanical, photocopying, recording, scanning, or otherwise without written permission from the publisher. It is illegal to copy this book, post it to a website, or distribute it by any other means without permission.*

*This novel is entirely a work of fiction. The names, characters and incidents portrayed in it are the work of the author's imagination. Any resemblance to actual persons, living or dead, events or localities is entirely coincidental.*

*First edition*

*This book was professionally typeset on Reedsy. Find out more at reedsy.com*

*To Hans Christian Andersen*
*Your story was wonderful, but the ending kinda sucked. So I changed it.*

*To Jane Austen*
*It is a truth universally acknowledged... Pride and Prejudice is amazing.*

# Contents

| | |
|---|---:|
| Chapter 1 | 1 |
| Chapter 2 | 6 |
| Chapter 3 | 14 |
| Chapter 4 | 30 |
| Chapter 5 | 39 |
| Chapter 6 | 46 |
| Chapter 7 | 53 |
| Chapter 8 | 62 |
| Chapter 9 | 70 |
| Chapter 10 | 80 |
| Chapter 11 | 87 |
| Chapter 12 | 97 |
| Chapter 13 | 106 |
| Chapter 14 | 114 |
| Chapter 15 | 127 |
| Chapter 16 | 132 |
| Chapter 17 | 141 |
| Chapter 18 | 147 |
| Chapter 19 | 156 |
| Chapter 20 | 161 |
| Chapter 21 | 170 |
| Chapter 22 | 179 |
| *Epilogue* | 191 |
| *Her Cursed Apple: Chapter 1* | 202 |

| | |
|---|---|
| *Also by Eliza Prokopovits* | 210 |
| *About the Author* | 211 |

# Chapter 1

Arielle would never have found the human if it hadn't been for Nonette's stories. Nonette was ancient, possibly as old as the sea itself, and she could talk with animals. Today she'd been telling Arielle of horses and of great wooden boxes humans rode into the water and of the most splendid palace with creamy towers. Sometimes her stories came from seals, or from whales who brought word of distant places, but today's tales were brought by the gulls that circled the human town. Nonette knew that Arielle loved stories, and she always saved the best for her eager young visitor.

Arielle had been visiting Nonette every day for longer than she could remember. She lived in a large cave in the chalk reef not far from Arielle's own, and she'd been the nearest thing to family that the girl had had. If Nonette remembered Arielle's parents—and she must, she remembered everything—it was the one story she never told. Arielle didn't mind being alone. She liked her solitude. But it would have been nice to have someone to belong to, maybe even someone to share a resemblance with. Arielle's few other friends all looked like their families: they had the same hair, whether brown or gray-green or copper-gold, and the same skin tone across their arms and torsos, and the same color scales covering their tails. Arielle alone had deep red hair and eyes the blue of a tropical lagoon—not that she'd ever been to the tropics, but she'd met a dolphin once with Nonette, and the dolphin had commented. And no one else's tail was quite the same old-copper green. Nonette didn't resemble anyone else, either, with her quicksilver hair and scales and even eyes, which unnerved Arielle's other friends so much they stopped visiting with her. But Arielle liked that Nonette didn't belong with anyone; it gave her a sense of camaraderie that they were both alone together.

So Arielle went to visit Nonette every day, usually bringing something along to share for breakfast. And Nonette almost always had a new story of some sort, even if it was just a joke from the starlings about humans who couldn't swim and so had to be carried into the water by other humans. Arielle laughed at the ridiculousness of the notion. To not be able to swim! Well, that wasn't so very odd, given their disappointing lack of tails, the poor things. And she supposed, thinking it over later, that it wasn't unnatural for them to *wish* to swim, even if they couldn't. So perhaps it was a sign of ingenuity that they found a way to enjoy the water despite their shortcomings. Still, Arielle couldn't help but laugh and pity them.

Nonette's stories, far from assuaging Arielle's natural curiosity, intrigued her. She thought of the humans often. She thought of the valiant battles that had been fought aboard ships, though she couldn't quite figure out what the commotion was all *for*, and of the humans who would battle each other one on one for love or revenge or amusement. She'd heard of humans moving to music, in a way that one seal described as beautiful but a nearby gull mocked mercilessly. Arielle was good with animals—they found her and played around her nearly as much

# CHAPTER 1

as they did with Nonette—but she never could decide if it was only because they recognized her as Nonette's friend or if she had a gift of her own. And they never spoke to her.

Sometimes she wished that she could understand the animals too, that she could hear the stories firsthand. But more often, she wished to see for herself.

No one went close to the shore. It wasn't safe, what with boats and fishing nets and those silly not-swimmers. Nonette only surfaced to speak to the gulls and starlings as they returned to their nests at night. But Arielle wanted so badly to see the magnificent palace, and it would be too dark to see it at night. So one day, after sharing breakfast with Nonette, instead of finding her friends or seeking out new, unexplored sections of coastline, Arielle swam toward the human town.

She kept her distance, of course, surfacing well out from the pebble beach because it was low tide and the humans would be farther from shore. Horses pulled boxes into the water, just like Nonette's seagulls had said. Arielle giggled to watch them. There were humans, too, just dark specks in the distance. The buildings on shore were harder for her to see clearly from this far out. She waited for the tide to go in so she could get a better look.

A cluster of large rocks stood off the shore, fully exposed by the low tide, but they would soon be covered and would provide a good vantage point. Arielle swam slowly toward them, watching as the water began to lap around the base of the nearest, and then the next. As she drew closer, she saw a human figure climbing on the rocks. He used his hands and feet to scale the sides, his movements almost crablike but much more graceful. Arielle was fascinated. Who knew that legs could be so useful? And so she was watching when his leg twisted oddly under him and he collapsed with a cry, slipping from his precarious perch.

Without considering the risks, Arielle swam closer. Keeping the rocks between herself and the shore, she sought a clear view of the human. He'd fallen between two of the rocks, wedged awkwardly in a crevice. His head lolled to one side. Arielle wondered if he'd hit it against the rock when he'd fallen. She studied the rising water. The rocks would be fully submerged at high tide; they were half submerged now. An unconscious man would drown, regardless of his swimming abilities.

Arielle could hear the admonishments of her friends' parents, commanding them to mind their own business and leave the humans to *theirs*, to keep their distance for the safety of all. But this man wasn't safe, and Arielle couldn't leave him to die, not when she was the only one who knew where he was and could help him.

She hovered nearby as the tide rose, finding a space in the lee of one of the rocks, where she was still hidden from shore but wouldn't be battered by the waves. The man would be immovable for her until he was nearly underwater. Soon enough, however, the water reached his chest, and Arielle seized her chance. She swam up from below, shoving until she had loosened him from his position. Awkwardly, she lay him to float on his back while she came underneath him and linked her arms through his. Fortunately, the incoming tide shoved them toward the shore so that Arielle didn't have to drag all his weight. A few hard tail-flicks brought them to the shallows.

There was no good place to leave him. Most of the other humans had abandoned their non-swimming; evening was falling, and the air was cool. For a split second, Arielle regretted that she hadn't seen the palace spires before the sun set. Then

## CHAPTER 1

the man groaned and struggled, and she let go. She shoved him a little farther up the beach, careful not to scrape herself on the pebbles. He half raised himself on one arm and opened his eyes.

For the first time, Arielle really looked at him. His hair was dark, as were his eyes, which blinked in unfocused confusion. His features were firm and handsome, and Arielle felt a rush of emotion she'd never felt before. She'd heard of love at first sight in Nonette's stories, and she was sure to her core that this must be it. This human man was the most appealing thing she'd ever seen, strong and beautiful, and she stared. His eyes turned to her, half-focused, and he stared too. Then his eyes closed, and his head lolled back, and she had to shove him hard again to keep him high enough on the beach to keep his face out of the water.

Voices shouted from up the beach. Arielle darted backward in alarm. Other humans were coming, but they had to go around the big wooden horse-drawn boxes that were parked by the path; they hadn't seen her. She slipped back to the deeper water where she'd be hidden, but she couldn't leave without making sure they found him. If they didn't, he'd still be at risk from the tide.

Several figures came into sight, crying out and running toward Arielle's rescued human. She watched as they picked him up, carrying him between them away from the waves. Arielle continued to watch until they'd carried him out of sight. Then she dove back below the surface, riding the current toward her reef cave.

# Chapter 2

Arielle brought breakfast to Nonette the next morning as usual, but instead of launching into a new tale of wonder, Nonette studied Arielle silently. It was uncomfortable to be examined by that silver gaze, and Arielle fidgeted.

At length, Nonette said, "Do *you* have a story for *me* today?"

Arielle knew that someone—a fish, a gull, a seahorse, a mollusk—had seen her rescue yesterday. It was no good denying it. So she told Nonette the story, leaving out no details, and trying to imbue it with the same sense of the incredible that her ageless friend used.

When she'd finished, Nonette continued to watch her, expressionless.

"Please don't tell," Arielle said, when she'd again grown uncomfortable. "My lack of parents will not excuse me from blame, I know. I shouldn't have done it, but I couldn't *not*."

"I won't tell," Nonette said quietly. "You did what you must. But I think you will not be quite the same after this."

Arielle's mouth fell open in surprise. Anyone else would have told her to put it from her mind. But she couldn't, and she already felt the change Nonette predicted. How could Nonette *know*?

## CHAPTER 2

Arielle stayed away from the shore that day, purposefully giving it a wide berth. But she couldn't erase the handsome face that kept appearing before her mind's eye. She couldn't deny the wish to see him again, to see if he had recovered from his extended time in the cold water. He probably wouldn't remember her—head injuries were like that, even among the people of the sea—but the way he'd stared…. Had he felt the same sense of falling that she had?

The next day, she swam back to the shore as if drawn by some indomitable force. She kept her distance, studying the tiny specks of humans, unable to see from that far if one was *her* human. Several fish darted playfully around her, and she gave up watching to play with them. She came again the day after, venturing a little closer at high tide to see the palace—a decadent confection of a building that both amused and delighted her. Before a week was out, Arielle had made it a habit of watching the humans. They were awkward and graceless, but still they fascinated her.

And then came the night of the music.

People were gathered in a wide open area beyond the beach. Arielle could get glimpses of them as she swam closer in the rising tide. The strains of music carried across the water like a murmuration of starlings, swooping and gliding and echoing over the waves. Arielle stayed to listen, dumbstruck. She barely became aware of the tide turning before she was stranded in a shallow pool to wait for its return.

The music haunted her dreams.

Nonette's stories were no longer enough. She wanted to know more about these people who lived on land, wanted to know how they made music that melted the soul. Wanted to hear their stories and live those stories with them. And, always, she wanted to see that one beautiful face again.

At last, one evening, she saw him. She had been about to turn for home when she threw a last look across the beach, and there he was. There were others with him, talking and laughing together, but he stood looking out across the water, as if he were looking for something.

Arielle knew with her whole being that he was looking for her. He'd seen her in that brief moment, and he was hoping for a glimpse of her in the same way she'd been looking for him. Her heart reached out to him, wishing she could swim closer. But she was not lost to caution. His friends must not see her. She twitched her head, hoping the sun would catch her brilliantly rosy hair and draw his eye, but the sun was casting a ruby glow across the whole scene, and she was invisible in it. She watched until he turned and walked away.

Nonette didn't tell Arielle a story the next day. "You *have* changed," she said instead. "I had hoped I was wrong."

Arielle shook her head. "I knew you weren't. They're just so… fascinating," she pleaded with her friend to understand. "I wish there were some way I could be human, if only for a day."

Nonette sighed. "I shouldn't tell you this, but it may lead to less harm than you would cause if I didn't."

She hesitated, and Arielle burst, "Tell me what?"

"There's someone who could possibly grant your wish. A Fae of the sea. He… he can be found sometimes at the farthest reaches of the chalk reef, though there's no telling when or where."

"How will I know him?" Arielle was already moving toward the doorway.

"You'll know," Nonette said. "But I beg you to consider carefully. Nothing comes without price."

## CHAPTER 2

Arielle sagged. "But I have nothing."

"You needn't fear that. He'll find something to take in exchange if he chooses to grant your request."

Arielle left, directing her path toward the outskirts of the reef. There was no doubt in her mind that she'd give anything to be human.

\*\*\*

Arielle saw no one as she swam the reef that day or the next. She couldn't watch the humans and search for the Faerie on the same day—the distance was too great to swim back and forth. So she alternated days, drawn to keep observing the town but unwilling to give up hope of finding a way to join them. This went on for weeks. Nonette made no further mention of the Fae or the change in Arielle, but she looked sadly at her oblivious young friend.

One day, Arielle saw someone swimming when she reached the edge of the reef. She didn't notice him at first—his skin was the color of the chalk seabed, and his hair was like fronds of purple kelp. He blended in with the reef life as if he belonged there, as if he'd always been there and she'd simply never noticed him in all the times she'd swum out this way.

His eyes flicked to her—bottomless dark pools of frigid water—and he began to swim away.

"Oh, no, please!" she called after him. "Wait!"

He waited for her to catch up to him. As Arielle came alongside him, she understood what Nonette had meant: she had no doubt that this person was fae. He looked enough like other sea people, with a silver-scaled tail and a broad bare chest, but there was also something extra about him, something perfect and unnatural.

"What do you want, child?" His voice held the crash of waves and the song of whales. Arielle shivered.

"I want to be human," she said softly. "Can you make it so?"

He laughed. "I can, but I don't see why I should. What would you want to be human for? Isn't the sea a beautiful place?"

"Oh, it is," Arielle agreed. "But I think land is beautiful too, and music and dancing and—oh, I don't know what else. But I *want* to know, do you see?"

His eyes narrowed. "You've met a human, haven't you, child?"

Arielle nodded. "I rescued him from drowning. We didn't speak, but I felt…" She suddenly remembered to whom she was talking, and she didn't want to share her innermost thoughts with the Fae.

"You wish to know more of *him*, I see."

"Not just him. Everyone. Every*thing*," Arielle protested.

He considered her thoughtfully. "Very well. I will tell you the terms. You will think them over for one week, and if you still wish to be human, you will meet me here."

"Yes, please."

"You would become human for a year and a day from the time you are changed. If you wish the change to become permanent, you must marry your human true love within that time."

Arielle thought about this. She knew little of magic, but she knew there was always a limit, always a cost. She nodded slowly. "What else?"

"There is no guarantee that the human you met will feel about you the way you do about him. It is a hazard of love that it may not be returned. Your heart may be broken."

Arielle remembered how she'd seen her human looking out to sea, searching for her. How could he not return her love?

## CHAPTER 2

But she said, "I understand."

"Understand also that if he does not, and if you do not marry your true love within a year and a day, you cannot return to the way you are now." Her eyes widened, and his brow raised in challenge as he went on. "Once magic has given you a full transformation, you cannot go back. You will not get a second attempt at being human, either. The best I could offer would be to finish your life as a seal or dolphin."

"Oh."

"I can set you up well for life with the humans—you will understand their language in all its forms, and you will be delivered to them in a way to ensure your well-being and care—but you will remember nothing of your current life."

"Nothing?" Arielle stared at him. Not Nonette? Not the creatures of the reef? Not swimming and diving with friends?

"Nothing. Your past is the price you must pay to change your future. It ensures that the sea remains safe from the humans."

Arielle hesitated, then nodded. She understood this: if someone were to spread tales of all the life just offshore, the humans would come exploring and, in the process, destroying the beautiful world beneath the waves.

"These are the terms?" she asked.

He nodded.

"I have a week?"

He nodded again. "Come to this place and call for me."

"What is your name?"

His mouth twitched in a private joke. "Humans have called me Poseidon. That is as good a name as any."

"Thank you," Arielle said. "I will return next week."

"Think carefully, child. Count the cost before you decide."

Arielle nodded and swam away, eager to have solitude to

think it all over. She wanted to be with the humans, but those terms! She'd hoped for a week on land, or a month, not a lifetime. And certainly not a year that ended with her finishing her life as a dolphin. Granted, the dolphin she'd met with Nonette had been the most carefree creature she'd met, and it had traveled farther than anyone she knew, so perhaps life as a dolphin wouldn't be terrible. But to become one would mean that she had failed, rejected by the human she wanted. Heartbroken. She'd forget everything she knew and treasured, wagering all her future on a hope and a dream. Was it enough? Was *he* enough, the one with the beautiful face?

Arielle spent the rest of the day lost in thought. She skipped breakfast with Nonette the next morning and spent the day haunting the rocks off the shore, watching for one precious human. But they were all precious in their way, and even though she didn't see him, she enjoyed watching the rest. The next morning, Nonette told her stories from the creatures of the reef. Reminded of all she was missing and all she'd forget, Arielle played on the reef with her friends that day and the next. They teased her at first about disappearing so often but soon let it drop. She had lovely days with them, but there was a distance between them that hadn't been there before. Arielle had missed out on adventures and inside jokes, and her friends knew nothing of the human world that filled her heart and mind. Far from convincing her to stay on the reef, Arielle's explorations with the other young sea people only showed her how much less she belonged than ever. She had no family, and she suspected that, after the first shock, no one but Nonette would truly miss her.

When the week was up, Arielle swam out to the edge of the reef. She'd hugged Nonette goodbye that morning, though she didn't say why, confident that her old friend would know where she'd gone when she failed to return.

"Poseidon?" she called when she reached the place where she'd met him before.

The Fae appeared before her, and she couldn't decide whether he hadn't been there and then was, or whether he'd always been there but was so camouflaged that she couldn't see him until he moved. He surveyed her with unreadable eyes.

"You have considered the terms?"

"I have," Arielle said, wishing her voice didn't tremble as she spoke. "I still want to be human."

"Very well, child. Take one last look at the home you will forget."

Arielle obediently turned from him to cast her gaze over the reef, smiling at how the late morning sun danced through the water and brightened the anemones and lazily drifting fronds of kelp. She had just caught sight of a lobster climbing from its hiding place when everything went black and she knew no more.

# Chapter 3

She heard the waves first, gently rushing upon the pebbles. It was a calm, peaceful sound, and she was content to lie and listen. Eventually, the pebbles beneath her grew uncomfortable, and she opened her eyes and pushed herself onto one elbow. Her head swam, and she lay back down, but she kept her eyes open. The pebbles nearest her head were brown and gray and white, smoothed by the ocean into curious shapes. They were pleasant to look at, so she looked. A gull hopped from spot to spot nearby, alternating searching for food left behind by the tide and eyeing her with interest.

"I'm not food," she croaked at it. She cleared her throat, swallowed, her mouth dry and tasting too much like salt. "But I wish you luck."

The gull tilted its head and squawked at her, a loud cry that made her flinch.

After another minute or two, she risked raising her head again, propping it on one hand. Now she could see the waves lapping at the beach a good distance away. Nearer at hand, bits of seaweed and tiny creatures dried out in the sun, stranded by the high tide, dinner for her gull and the others that also hunted their next meal.

## CHAPTER 3

She wore a dress of an indeterminate shade of green, rather tattered at the edges and clinging damply to her. She must have been stranded by the tide as well.

Frowning, she pushed herself up to seated, hugging her knees and resting her head on them as the world around her sloshed and steadied. From where she sat, she could see a handful of wooden structures—massive boxes on wheels, with horses hitched to one end—some on the beach, some in the water. They were curious things, and figures moved around them. She watched with interest as one of the boxes in the water was towed back up the beach to stop not far away. A large woman in a sopping-wet dress led the horse. A smaller woman—dry—met them above the high tide line and climbed into the end of the box, which opened for her, then closed again. After a few minutes, the box opened again and the woman came out, reaching to assist someone else out. This someone was delicate and slight, with white hair twisted neatly atop her head. Her clothing was dry, but there was a bundle carried by the younger woman that may have contained wet garments.

It took several moments before they noticed the girl watching them, fascinated, from farther along the beach. They conferred together briefly, before the younger woman approached.

"Good afternoon, dear." She crouched near the girl. "Are you lost? Are you well?"

"I think I am—both of those things."

"Where is your family?"

"I don't know. I…" Two faces came into her mind, one pale as chalk with deep purple hair, the other human and tanned with dark hair and dark, beautiful eyes. The word *family* didn't seem to apply to either one. She thought harder, but came up with only a feeling of solitude and loneliness. "I don't think I have one."

"Where are you from?"

She shook her head but stopped quickly as the world sloshed again. "I don't know."

"Do you have a name?"

"Arielle." She was relieved to have an answer for that, at least.

"What a lovely name, Arielle. Have you a surname?"

Arielle frowned, again coming up with emptiness. "Just Arielle."

The woman smiled kindly. "I'm Olivia Farley, and my aunt, Lady Priscilla Farley, is just over there. I believe it would be best if you came home with us for now, to get cleaned up and have something to eat. Could you do that?"

Arielle's stomach rumbled at the thought of food. "Yes, please."

Miss Farley helped her to her feet, allowing Arielle to lean on her shoulder as her head spun. "You've been through rather a lot, haven't you, dear?" Her bright eyes were green, and she was just the same height as Arielle, which made it easier for them to walk back up the beach. Arielle studied her out of the corner of her eye, taking in the delicate nose, high cheekbones, and curling dark blonde hair. Lady Priscilla, she saw when they approached, had the same nose and grass-green eyes, but she was half a head shorter.

"Aunt Prissy, this is Arielle," Miss Farley said, stopping before the older lady. "She has no memory of a home or family, so I thought it best that she stay with us for the day. Poor thing needs a bite to eat."

"Well, of course she does, spending goodness knows how long in the water and sun." Lady Priscilla's voice was light

## CHAPTER 3

and cheerful, and her face crinkled every which way when she smiled. Arielle liked her immediately. "You'll stay with us, my dear, while we search for your family."

"I don't think I have one, ma'am," Arielle said slowly. "I don't remember, but I... I think I was alone."

"Oh, you poor dear," Lady Priscilla said. "You are most definitely coming with us, then. We've plenty of room, and you can stay as long as you like."

Arielle thanked them both, and the three of them treaded slowly up the beach toward the road. Miss Farley and Lady Priscilla kept up a steady stream of talk as they walked, so that Arielle was too distracted to pay much attention to where they were walking. Before they'd reached the front door of an elegant brick house, the ladies had decided that Arielle would eat first, then have a bath.

Arielle submitted without argument as the ladies ushered her into a bright room with a table and chairs and rang the bell for tea.

"With cold meats and a decent spread, James," Lady Priscilla instructed the footman. "This poor child needs nourishment."

The footman looked at the poor child in question with astonishment before bowing and vanishing in the direction of the kitchen.

"No doubt all the staff will know about you before the tea arrives," Miss Farley remarked to Arielle as she helped her into a chair and then pulled one up to sit beside her. "But they're all good souls."

Food was brought, and Arielle felt better about eating when she saw that the others were piling plates for themselves as well.

"Sea bathing always makes me hungry," Lady Priscilla said,

pouring tea. "So do surprises." She beamed at Arielle. "Although I think you're the pleasantest surprise I've had these many years. I've had a thought, my dear, and I wonder how you'll take it."

When the older woman paused, Miss Farley shifted impatiently in her chair. "Do tell us, Aunt Prissy! You can't say something like that and leave us wondering."

Lady Priscilla grinned at her niece. "Patience, Livvie, dear, I'm still thinking. And what I'm thinking is that if Miss Arielle here has no family and no idea where home is, then maybe we can offer her ours. I mean, if she's not opposed to it, I can adopt her as my ward, and she can live here with us."

Arielle stared at her, wide eyed. The idea of a home, of belonging, called to her with overwhelming strength and made her forget that these women were strangers she'd met only minutes ago. "Oh, would you?"

Miss Farley clapped her hands. "That *is* a splendid idea. But how does one go about adopting a ward?"

"I'll see Mr. Stearns about it tomorrow. An attorney's got to be good for something, hasn't he?"

"Thank you, Lady Priscilla," Arielle stammered. Her mind slowly caught up to her emotions, and she realized the burden this family would be taking on. But she still couldn't say no. "You're too good."

"Now, now, none of that." Lady Priscilla waved her hand. "You're family now. Call me Aunt Prissy like Livvie does—I've never been one to hold with formalities at home."

"No, nor I," Olivia Farley said. "What fun this will be! Two old spinsters like we are don't often get the chance to launch a young lady into society. We'll have to take her to Madame Morris tomorrow, of course—it won't do for her to borrow my gowns forever. They're too dowdy for such a pretty young thing."

Arielle frowned at her. "What do you mean—launching into society?"

"Oh, just introducing you about town. There are an abundance of unwritten rules and customs about it, but that's what it boils down to."

That wasn't so frightening, Arielle decided. The handsome face with dark hair and eyes returned to her mind. She didn't know who he was, but her heart told her that he was important to her. Maybe being introduced into society would bring her to him.

"I'd like that," she said. "I hope it's not too much trouble for you." She frowned at Olivia as she recalled something else the woman had said. "'*Old* spinsters'—you can't be so very old."

Olivia laughed. "I'm on the wrong side of forty, dear, but I don't mind. Living with Aunt Prissy keeps me young." She glanced at Arielle's plate. "If you're finished, let's see about that bath."

An hour later, Arielle was clean, dry, and dressed in a borrowed nightgown. She could see from the light through the window that it was still early, but she was exhausted from the day. She allowed Olivia to bundle her into bed in the spare bedroom, and to her surprise, fell asleep within minutes.

Arielle woke in the morning to the sight of a maid opening the curtains and laying out a dress on the back of a chair for her. "Good morning, miss. I'm Lindsay, the Farleys' abigail. Would you like help to dress?"

"Yes, please," Arielle said, sitting up in bed with a yawn and wondering what an abigail was. From the look of things, she was a maid who helped with a lady's wardrobe. Or maybe

Arielle was a special case because she was so new. Arielle had half expected this all to be a dream. It certainly felt like one. The lack of context for her life—who she was, where she came from—was uncomfortable and lent a surreal quality to her present experiences. But the Farleys had been beyond welcoming, and she was grateful.

Lindsay helped her dress in the borrowed gown. It was a little loose in the bodice—Olivia had a fuller figure than Arielle did—but it fit well enough. There were undergarments and stockings as well. Arielle didn't mind the undergarments, but the stockings felt strange and constricting on her feet, and she wished she could go without.

When she was wearing everything Lindsay required, the woman made her sit on a stool while she braided and pinned her hair. "Your hair is such an exquisite rose," Lindsay murmured as she worked. "One could create art with hair like this. But Miss Farley was explicit: a serviceable style for the day because you'll be spending the morning with the modiste." She placed a final pin and tucked a lock out of the way. "There."

Arielle's neck felt wobbly, the weight and balance of her hair piled atop her head feeling strange and unfamiliar.

"You'll get used to it, miss," Lindsay said with a smile. "And if I may say, welcome to the Farley family."

Lindsay curtsied and excused herself. Instead of following her and finding her way to breakfast, Arielle stayed where she was. It was an odd sensation, but she felt she was learning a great deal about her former life simply by experiencing things. For one, she was positive she'd never worn her hair like this before. Stockings, crisp linen sheets, and the cold chicken and salads from dinner the night before—all new. She thought hard, trying to remember anything she could about her past.

## CHAPTER 3

The face of the man she wanted to meet, though extremely handsome, told her nothing. It simply set her heart aflutter but brought no new memories. Perhaps meeting him in person would help her recall something.

Her memory of the other face, the one with the unnaturally pale skin and deepest-darkest-ocean eyes—what an odd description to use, she thought, and yet it fit—gave her more. It gave her a strong sense of magic, that there was a reason for her absent past. She heard snatches of words in a voice that reminded her of the waves on the beach yesterday. *Marry. True love. A year and a day.*

Arielle shivered. Were these the rules of the magic that bound her? Why must she marry? And what happened if she missed the deadline? How long had it been since the strange person had spoken those words?

She stood and resolved to put those worries from her mind for now. The introductions Olivia Farley was planning were bound to bring her to the one she wished to see. To do that, she had to see the modiste today, and before that, breakfast. Her stomach rumbled in confirmation that food was the first order of business.

She found her way to the dining room, where the two Farley ladies were seated at the table, already starting on tea and toast.

"Good morning, dear," Lady Priscilla greeted her. "Did you sleep well?"

"Very well, thank you." Arielle took the seat next to her. Soon plates of eggs and sausage and bacon were brought, and more toast.

When they'd finished, Olivia said, "You didn't get to see much of the house last night, Arielle, so I thought we might show you around quickly before we go out."

It wasn't a large house, but everything was so new to Arielle, and she was grateful for the offer. The top floor contained three bedrooms, which she'd seen on her way to her own room last night. Besides the dining room, the first floor also contained a drawing room at the very front of the house and a small family parlor at the back. Arielle liked the parlor. It was furnished with taste but with comfort in mind before style. The chairs and sofa were plush and piled with embroidered pillows. A luxurious carpet covered the floor, and the walls were painted an amber-gold that made Arielle feel like she was caught in a cozy summer sunset. The windows were open to admit a salty breeze off the channel.

The drawing room, on the other hand, while it was decorated with as much taste as the parlor, was less comfortable. There were fewer pillows, and the rug, while finely crafted, was less plush. The furniture was made with more wood than cushion. It was a place for impressing visitors, not for spending a cozy evening. A small pianoforte sat in one corner.

Arielle was whisked away for one final stop in the kitchen, where she was introduced to the rest of the staff. There were four servants employed by the family—Lindsay, the abigail, whom Arielle had met that morning, and James, the footman, plus Mrs. Little, the cook, and Mary, the housemaid. The kitchen was at the back of the house, and it ought to have seemed dark and cramped, given that two small windows opened onto the alley behind the house and the room was crowded with a large worktable, shelves, a stove, and various other cooking implements. But the walls were bright from being recently whitewashed and the windows were clean and let in the morning sunlight. The door stood wide open to allow in what breeze would come. Everything in the kitchen was tidy and organized, and the gleaming copper pots reflected back the light.

It was a pleasant room, despite the heat from the stove. Mary, the young housemaid, bustled about, washing up after breakfast, while Mrs. Little mixed something in a bowl with strong strokes of a large spoon. She paused and used the back of her wrist to swipe wisps of hair from her glistening face before curtsying to Arielle.

"Pleasure to have you here, miss," she said. "You let me know if there's any food you like in particular, and I'll see that you have it."

"Thank you," Arielle said, still gazing around the room in wonder. There were so many unfamiliar things in this kitchen. "Everything has been delicious so far."

A furry body slunk up to Arielle and rubbed around her ankles, releasing a low rumble as it did. Arielle crouched to get a closer look, reaching automatically to stroke between the creature's ears. It was mostly white, with four black feet, a black spot on one shoulder, and another on its long tail. It looked up at her with the sweetest, funniest face, all white but with black markings beneath its nose that made it look like it had a mustache. She giggled. It blinked bright yellow-green eyes at her, and she bit her lip, afraid she'd offended it. Instead, it pressed its head more firmly against her hand and rumbled louder.

A part of her mind supplied that this was a cat, but she was quite certain she'd never met one before. She'd remember something as loving and adorable as this little thing.

"Well, would you look at that," she heard Mrs. Little say. She glanced up at the cook, who was watching in amusement. "I wasn't sure Hissy was capable of making friends."

"Hissy?"

"His name was originally Hessy," Olivia explained, eyeing the cat but keeping her distance. "Because he looks like he's wearing Hessian boots. But he doesn't much like anyone here, so he earned his grumpy nickname."

"Why is he here, then, if he doesn't get along with anyone?" Arielle asked, still petting the purring feline.

"He gets plenty of food between scraps and hunting, and I appreciate that he keeps the place free of mice." The cat glanced up at Mrs. Little who gave him a small nod. "We may not be overly friendly, but the arrangement works."

"I have a hard time believing you're so very grumpy," Arielle murmured to the cat. "I'll be your friend, if you like."

Mrs. Little chuckled, and Olivia shook her head. After another moment with her new friend, Arielle stood, knowing that she was supposed to be leaving with her human friends shortly. But she was distracted by what Mrs. Little was doing. She was pouring what she'd been mixing in the bowl into a smallish rectangular pan. The yellowish stuff oozed from the bowl, wet and thick and smooth but somehow entirely unappealing.

"What are you making?" Arielle stepped closer, fascinated.

"Pound cake, miss. It'll be served with tea when you return."

Arielle wasn't sure what a pound cake was, and judging by the glop she could see in the pan, she couldn't say that she looked forward to it. She made a noncommittal noise and nodded, then followed Olivia out of the kitchen. They found Lady Priscilla back in the dining room, folding up a letter she'd just finished reading. Within minutes, they'd supplied Arielle with a borrowed bonnet and gloves, and the three walked out to Brighton Place to see Madame Morris.

## CHAPTER 3

The modiste greeted Lady Priscilla like an old friend and gushed her delight at her ladyship's new ward. Arielle hadn't given much thought, up to this point, about what her new wardrobe would entail, but she was soon overwhelmed. Morning dresses, walking dresses, ballgowns, evening gowns, night gowns. Not to mention hats and headdresses to go with every variety, and gloves, slippers, reticules, spencers, and pelisses to complete each ensemble. Once the number and type of gowns were decided, they had to decide on fabrics: jaconet and sarcenet, cotton and crepe, twilled or sprigged or striped... Arielle's head spun. Olivia and Madame Morris agreed that all the gowns ought to be in shades of green and blue, to emphasize Arielle's eyes while offsetting her hair, aside from two obligatory white ballgowns.

Madame Morris then took out her measuring tape while her assistant brought out a pair of ready-made gowns that should fit with light alteration. At this, Lady Priscilla took her leave to pay a call on her attorney down the street. She knew what Arielle wouldn't discover until later: this fitting would last hours. She stood on a stool to be measured, then changed into the first new dress, which Madame Morris pinned until Arielle couldn't move without getting pricked. Somehow, they extricated her in order to do it again with the second. Aunt Prissy returned in a cheerful humor to find an exhausted Arielle just changing back into her borrowed gown while the modiste assured Olivia that those two gowns would be ready within three days, with the others to be sent along as they were finished.

Taking Arielle's arm in hers, Olivia told her brightly that there was still quite a lot of shopping to do in order to prepare for her introduction to society. It would wait until tomorrow, however. Aunt Prissy ought to rest after such a busy morning. Arielle was grateful, both for the promised rest and Olivia's tact in refraining from pointing out how wan Arielle had become. When they returned to the Farley's house on Marine Parade, Aunt Prissy retired to her room to lie down. Olivia went in search of Mrs. Little to discuss dinner, and Arielle was left on her own in the parlor. She flopped onto the sofa and rested her head against the pillow. Her neck was stiff from the unaccustomed weight of balancing her hair pinned high rather than hanging long. She closed her eyes, content to just sit after the overwhelming morning. But she wasn't sleepy, and after a few minutes she opened her eyes again and looked around the room. It was a nice room, cozy and welcoming, and it made her feel just as much at home as the women who inhabited it. Her eyes fell on a book that lay on the table nearby, and she picked it up. *Sense and Sensibility*, declared the title. With nothing else to do, Arielle opened it and began to read.

She was thoroughly engrossed when Olivia tentatively pushed the door open and peeked inside before joining Arielle on the sofa. "I thought you might be sleeping. Do you like the book?"

Arielle nodded, holding her page with her finger. "I feel like I could be friends with Elinor," she admitted, blushing. "Is that what reading usually does?"

Olivia grinned. "With some books it does. I'm glad you like it. Mr. Donaldson at the Marine Library recommended it last time I went. Aunt Prissy prefers poetry, and I usually like heroic tales of knights in shining armor. But someone else had borrowed *Le Morte d'Arthur*, so I had to try something new."

Arielle couldn't help smiling. "I don't think I've read either of those, but I look forward to it. If they're as good as this Miss

Austen, I expect I'll enjoy them a great deal."

Lady Priscilla joined them in time for tea, looking refreshed and as spritely as ever. Arielle was astonished when a slice of pound cake was handed to her on a plate, looking a bit like bread only denser. Her first bite told her that it was richer and sweeter too, and she closed her eyes to savor it.

Aunt Prissy was watching her with a twinkle of laughter in her gaze when she looked up again. "Do you like the pound cake, dear?"

Arielle laughed, blushing. "I do. I… I didn't expect to, after seeing what it looked like earlier. How…?" She wasn't sure how to complete the question.

"You saw it before it was baked," Olivia explained. "The batter is nothing like the final cake."

Arielle's blush deepened. This was probably something everyone knew. She felt like an idiot.

Aunt Prissy rested her hand on Arielle's. "Don't worry, dear. You're bound to experience all kinds of new things. Ask your questions without fear, and we'll be happy to answer them."

This made her feel a little better, though she hoped she wouldn't be constantly feeling as ignorant and silly as she did now.

After tea, the three took a short walk along Marine Parade. The cobbled street overlooked the beach on one side, and the other was lined with houses. Most of the houses were pressed up against each other with no space in between, and many of them were the same shade of pale limestone, though a few were painted or fronted with red brick. Front doors opened directly onto the street, separated only by a few steps or a short walkway. Arielle found the houses interesting, but her attention was drawn to the sunset over the water.

After their walk, they returned to the parlor. Her ladyship reached for her needlepoint, but Olivia stopped her.

"Aunt Prissy, I think we ought to begin teaching Arielle to dance, don't you?"

Arielle, who had picked up her book again, set it back down. "Dance?" Her mind supplied an image—a memory?—of watching people move gracefully together. Arielle's heart soared at the thought of doing that herself. She knew, somehow, that she loved music.

"Of course," Aunt Prissy said. "You'll be attending assemblies once you're fitted up."

Would the man with the beautiful face be at the assemblies? Would she be able to dance with him? Just that hope was enough to bring her to her feet.

She followed Olivia and Aunt Prissy to the drawing room, where they pushed chairs and couches against the wall to leave space in the middle of the floor.

Lady Priscilla settled herself at the pianoforte in the corner. "What shall we start with?"

"A reel or a circle dance?"

When they'd settled it between them to begin with one of several country dances, Olivia joined Arielle in the center of the floor and showed her the steps. They walked through them slowly, over and over, until Arielle got them right more often than not.

"Now with music," Olivia said.

Aunt Prissy began to play, slowly and simply, while they walked through the steps again. After a few times at that speed, Aunt Prissy picked up the tempo. Arielle at once tripped over her feet and forgot the order of the steps, falling into fits of giggles as she collided with Olivia and the two collapsed onto a chair in gales of laughter.

"That's enough for one night," Olivia hiccuped. "We'll sleep on it and try again tomorrow."

She was true to her word. The next day was spent shopping, with parcels of all their purchases to be delivered to the house that afternoon. After resting upon their return, they dined and then spent the evening in dancing lessons. Arielle remembered the steps better than she expected, and she didn't do so badly when Lady Priscilla played the music to tempo.

This began their habit of dancing in the evenings. Most of their lessons ended in fits of laughter, if they didn't begin with them.

# Chapter 4

Arielle woke the next morning to a low rumble beside her head. She opened her eyes to find a pair of yellow-green ones staring back at her. The purr redoubled, and Arielle smiled at Hessy as he stood, stretched, and then rubbed his head against her chin and cheek. The sound of his happiness vibrated through her, and she laughed softly, reaching to scratch behind his delicate pink ears. From this close, she could see that his nose was the same light pink, as was his tongue when he yawned. She marveled at his tiny but sharply pointed teeth and the whiskers that tickled her neck as he nuzzled her.

"You're a wonderful little creature," she murmured to him in awe. "Truly astonishing. You've probably made so few friends within the house because they don't see how remarkable you are."

This earned her a lick on the chin from his rough pink tongue. She giggled.

"Well, I think you're the sweetest little fellow I've ever met."

She didn't tell him that he was the only cat she'd ever met, though she was confident it was true. It was odd, she thought now, that when she'd met him yesterday, she'd known right away what he was despite his utter newness to her. It wasn't memory that supplied the name; it was something else. She wondered if it was more of that magic that hid her past from her, and she wondered what else she'd know without having experienced it before.

She gently dislodged Hessy, who had flopped over her shoulder and half of her chest to rest his head beneath her chin, and got up. She rang the bell for Lindsay to help her dress and arrange her hair. When she left the room, Hessy padded along down the stairs beside her, rubbing against her ankles once more before peeling off to head for the kitchen while Arielle joined the Farley ladies in the breakfast room.

The first two of Arielle's new dresses arrived that afternoon, and the following morning Lindsay helped her into in an emerald green walking dress, since her morning dresses had yet to arrive. She entered the breakfast room to delighted cheers from her guardian.

"You look lovely!" Lady Priscilla beamed. "That color becomes you so well, Ari, dear." She beckoned Arielle over and kissed both cheeks before waving her off to sit down to eat. "That settles it: we're paying morning calls today to introduce you."

Arielle's stomach clenched. Sensing Arielle's nerves, Olivia reached over and patted her hand. "Nothing to fear, dear. Just a few of Aunt Prissy's friends who would be offended if they didn't get to meet you before you take the assemblies by storm."

"They'll think you simply charming," Aunt Prissy reassured her. "And when *they* like you, everyone else will too. You'll be a hit."

Arielle didn't know what to expect from these visits, and uncertainty took most of her appetite away. After a few nibbles of toast, she gave up. She trusted her guardian, though, and reminded herself that Aunt Prissy's friends couldn't be too awful. She also knew that meeting new people was her only hope of finding the man with the face she remembered. So after breakfast she put on her new bonnet and gloves and walked out with Lady Priscilla and Olivia.

Their first call was only just down the street: Lady Caroline Hervey. She was a slight woman with a pleasant face and elegantly coiffed white hair. She looked to be about Lady Priscilla's age, if not a little older, and she rose to greet them with grace and warmth. Two other women were already there, and were introduced as Mrs. Goulding and Lady Shelley. Mrs. Goulding was a comfortable-looking woman who greeted Olivia and asked if she'd been to the library lately. This caused Olivia to choose the seat next to her, and they talked of books and the people they'd seen lately. Lady Shelley was younger than Arielle would have expected, no more than a decade older than herself, and dressed in the first mode of fashion. When Aunt Prissy introduced Arielle as her new ward, she was looked over with eager eyes and questioned her politely but implacably.

"No accomplishments?" Lady Caroline mused, on hearing that Arielle could not draw, paint, sing, or play the pianoforte, nor did she know any foreign languages or magical illusions. "That will be a hindrance, I'm afraid."

"Not at all, I'm sure," Lady Shelley protested. "Just look at the girl. Any man with eyes will be dangling after her. And to appear from nowhere like that. The wonder and novelty must be interesting to everyone who meets her."

Arielle didn't especially like being discussed as if she weren't present. And she wasn't sure if she wanted all manner of men to be interested in her. She only needed one—*the* one, her true

## CHAPTER 4

love to marry within a year.

After a few more minutes, Lady Shelley took her leave. "Sir John and I are only here for a few weeks before leaving for the continent," she told Aunt Prissy. "And there always seems to be something more to resolve before going to Paris."

When she'd departed, Mrs. Goulding turned to Arielle. "I do think, Miss Arielle, that you must be just the age of my Letitia. She's shopping with friends this morning, otherwise she would have come calling with me. I do think you'll hit it off as soon as you meet her. Would you allow me the pleasure of bringing her to call on you sometime?"

Arielle said politely that the pleasure would be hers. "I haven't met any young ladies of my own age yet, and I should be delighted to have a new friend."

They stayed for the standard half hour, then called at three more houses, only to leave Aunt Prissy's card in the owner's absence. "Well, we'll see them tomorrow," Aunt Prissy said philosophically. "If not at church, then at the promenade."

The promenade, they told Arielle, was when half of Brighton came out to walk about the Steine on Sunday evenings, culminating in tea at the Castle Tavern.

"It's always lovely to meet up with friends, though it's not as cozy as a drawing room chat," Olivia said.

Arielle found the Steine to be rather more crowded than she'd expected, when they began their next evening's sojourn. She and Olivia flanked Aunt Prissy, each with one of her arms tucked through their own. As they walked, Aunt Prissy told Arielle some of the gossip about the people they saw. "Granted, they're nothing to the types you'd see in London," she chuckled. "Beau Brummell, Lord Byron, Lady Caro Lamb, Lord Alvanley… You could fill a library with the stories I've heard about them."

"And don't forget Prinny." Olivia leaned in. "If he comes to the Pavilion this season, you may yet see him."

"Prinny?" Arielle asked.

"His Royal Highness, the Prince Regent," Aunt Prissy explained. "He loves Brighton and had the Pavilion built specially as his summer residence."

Arielle could see the elaborate peaks of the palace on the far side of the Steine. She had wondered who might live there, but she hadn't dared ask. It was still a matter of some embarrassment for her that she was so ignorant about seemingly everything.

They were interrupted by a cry and a wave from one of Aunt Prissy's friends. She towed the other two with her to greet the acquaintance, a stout woman in her sixth decade who clung lightly to her husband's arm. Arielle was presented to her and was subjected, to her alarm, to the same questioning she'd faced in Lady Caroline Hervey's drawing room about her origins and accomplishments. She was relieved when Aunt Prissy made their excuses, only to be hailed again a moment later to go through the same process.

After the fourth round of questioning, Arielle took Olivia aside while Lady Priscilla was listening to a long-winded friend regale her with her recent adventures.

"Livvie," she whispered, "I can't help feeling like I'm a failure without accomplishments. Could you teach me some?"

Olivia smothered a laugh. "Don't let it worry you, Ari. Accomplishments are more of a metric that interfering mamas can use to compare and judge each other's daughters. They are of little to no use in actual life, and a man of sense will know as much and love you anyway."

## CHAPTER 4

"But doesn't Aunt Prissy still play the pianoforte?"

"Yes, dear, but that's because she loves music, not because she needs to be accomplished. I can draw, sing, and speak French and Italian, but I've never once used those skills since my first few Seasons, before I came to live with Aunt Prissy." Seeing Arielle still looking unconvinced, she added, "If any of those things sounds like something you'd enjoy, I could teach you. And, who knows? Maybe you've simply forgotten. Sit down at the piano tomorrow and see what happens." She smiled encouragingly.

Arielle let the subject drop and walked with her guardians for another hour before repairing to the crowded tavern for tea. By the time they arrived home that evening, she was exhausted. She had seen and spoken to and been examined by more people than she had ever beheld in one place, she was certain. Each interaction left her drained a little more until all she could do was undress and collapse into bed.

The next morning, she went to the drawing room before breakfast and hesitantly sat down on the piano stool. Nothing about it felt familiar, and when she lifted the cover from the keys and played a single note, it didn't bring up any sudden burst of knowledge. She'd never played the pianoforte before in her life, she was sure. She sighed and closed the instrument, then went in to breakfast.

Aunt Prissy and Olivia had decided to stay home in case any of the friends they'd seen lately decided to return their calls this morning, so Arielle curled up in the parlor to finish *Sense and Sensibility* while it was quiet. She'd just closed the back cover and breathed a final sigh when James, the footman, knocked and announced that Mrs. and Miss Goulding were in the drawing room, and that Aunt Prissy was requesting her attendance.

Arielle rose and hurried to the other room. Mrs. Goulding and her daughter were seated on the sofa, and Miss Letitia Goulding rose to take Arielle's hand in greeting. She was tall and willowy, with golden curls that glowed in the light from the windows.

"Mama has told me so much about you," she said with a bright smile. "I do hope we'll be friends."

"I'm sure we shall be," Arielle said. She liked Miss Goulding's smile and easy manner.

She and Miss Goulding sat in chairs near each other. Aunt Prissy and Mrs. Goulding were already in conversation, and seeing this, Miss Goulding leaned closer and murmured, "We would have come earlier, but the milliner delivered my new hat just as we were leaving, and Mama insisted on seeing if it suited my pomona green walking dress as well as we'd hoped."

"Did it?" Arielle asked.

"Oh, yes, it suits perfectly. I can't wait to wear them together to the next promenade. Or perhaps a picnic. Don't you think picnics are the most delightful things?"

Arielle made a noncommittal sound. She couldn't remember having been on a picnic. Miss Goulding took it for assent and beamed at her. Arielle searched for something to say. "I confess, I'm glad you took the extra time to examine the hat, not only because I'm sure it will be very becoming. I was just finishing a book before you arrived, and I rather think I would have resented the interruption if you'd come when I had only three pages left!"

"What book?" Miss Goulding asked eagerly.

"*Sense and Sensibility*."

"Oh, I love Miss Austen's books. Have you read *Pride and*

*Prejudice* yet?"

"No, this was my first."

"You'll *adore* it, I'm sure. What about Mrs. Radcliffe, have you read any of hers?"

"I'm afraid not," Arielle said. "I'm still new here, and I haven't set foot in the library yet."

Miss Goulding expressed her shock and pressed her to visit the Marine Library the very next day to borrow *The Mysteries of Udolpho*. She continued to expound on her favorite novels, including *Camilla* and the controversial *Belinda*.

"I *am* glad the lending libraries here are so good," Miss Goulding said. "We came directly from town, you see, as soon as the Season there ended. Town is unbearably hot in the summer, and Mama thought a little sea-bathing would be just the thing. But Brighton is so very small a place in comparison. The balls and promenades are great fun, and the card parties, of course, but one often has to find one's own amusement here."

Arielle kept to herself how crowded and busy she'd found the tea and promenade the evening before. If this was "so very small a place," she had no desire ever to see London. She asked about Miss Goulding's experiences in town, and the other girl was more than happy to tell of all the larks she had gotten up to.

By the end of the visit, Letitia Goulding and Arielle had cemented their friendship by calling each other by their Christian names and had promised to seek each other out at the next ball at the Old Ship.

Aunt Prissy looked thoughtfully after their visitors when they left, saying to Arielle, "That girl's a diamond of the first water, and no mistake. I'm surprised she isn't engaged yet—girls with her looks, fortune, and accomplishments are usually snapped up in their first season."

"I'm glad she wasn't," Arielle said simply, "because then she wouldn't have come here, and I wouldn't have met her. She's a sweet girl, and I'm glad to have a friend. But she does talk a lot."

"Just like her mother." Aunt Prissy laughed.

"She recommended a great many books," Arielle said, "and she has done and seen so much more than I have…. I think."

"That's not such a bad thing. Look at it another way: you get the excitement of new experiences all the time. Poor Miss Goulding must often be bored or comparing current pleasures to past ones."

Arielle smiled. Lady Priscilla's optimism was boundless. "Do you have that same problem?" she asked.

"Oh, no, dear. I'm never bored. One cannot be bored when one has the ability to find amusement in the smallest things." Aunt Prissy smiled. "And you, Ari, are just the thing to keep me fresh. I feel like a young girl in my first season just walking through town with you."

Arielle laid a hand on Aunt Prissy's arm. "Thank you so much for taking me in."

"I wasn't fishing for gratitude, dear." Aunt Prissy patted Arielle's hand. "I'm quite glad we took you in as well. It hasn't even been a week, and I'm already fond of you." She leaned in and kissed Arielle's cheek. "You're a Farley now, like it or not."

"How could I not like it?"

"I haven't the foggiest notion." Lady Priscilla grinned. "To my mind, everyone ought to wish to be a Farley."

Arielle laughed.

# Chapter 5

The next morning, Arielle and Olivia ventured out to purchase a few small things, including ribbons and lace and strings of beads to wear to the ball at the Old Ship on Thursday. The first of Arielle's ball gowns had been delivered, and despite her protests that she couldn't perform all the dances confidently, Lady Priscilla and Olivia were both determined that this should be her debut event. Their hands full of small parcels, the two stopped last at the Marine Library. It was a large, green building with many-paned windows to let in the light and command an excellent view of the beach. Olivia returned the Austen book, and before long, they were leaving with a new book each: *Le Morte d'Arthur* for Olivia, having been returned just the day before, and the Mrs. Radcliffe story Miss Goulding had recommended. Arielle was distracted on the way back to Lady Priscilla's house, between excitement over a new book, nerves about Thursday's ball, and her persistent wonder at the beauty of the sea. No matter what the weather, she had yet to see the waves look anything but entrancing.

She was pondering this when she turned from the road and made her way up the steps.

"Ari!" Olivia called softly from the street. "Wrong house!"

Arielle glanced over her shoulder at Olivia, who was beckoning her, then looked back at the door she stood in front of. It was very like the Farleys', but it was definitely not the right one. She blushed and was just turning to rejoin her friend when the door in question opened and a man stepped out. He froze, startled, at the sight of her. Arielle gasped and stumbled down the steps, dropping her book and her parcels.

"Oh no," she squeaked, frantically bending down to gather everything, her face flaming.

"May I?" The gentleman descended the steps gracefully and crouched beside her, picking up what she couldn't reach and handing them to her.

By this time, Olivia had rushed over. "I beg your pardon, Lord Patrick. This is Aunt Prissy's new ward, Arielle Farley. She's still new to Brighton and mistook the house."

Arielle risked a peek at the man's face. He was young—perhaps six- or seven-and-twenty—and good looking, with light brown hair and gray eyes. "I'm so sorry to intrude," she managed in a whisper.

"Not at all." He smiled kindly. "You're welcome to accidentally come to my door any time."

He straightened and offered Arielle his hand. She took it and let him assist her to her feet. Standing, he wasn't much taller than she was, only a few inches. She looked to Olivia to extract her from the awkward moment.

Lord Patrick turned to Olivia as well. "Will I see you and your aunt at the Old Ship this week, Miss Farley?"

"You will," she agreed. "It will be Arielle's first ball in Brighton, and we're quite looking forward to it. Speaking of my aunt, however, we really should be getting back—she's probably been expecting us this hour."

Lord Patrick bowed. "Then I won't keep you. I'm honored

to make your acquaintance, Miss Arielle."

Arielle curtsied and murmured something not quite coherent about it being her pleasure before taking Olivia's arm and hurrying back to the street.

When they were out of earshot, Olivia whispered, "That was Lord Patrick Alexander, brother of the Duke of Marsham. He's the youngest brother and has always been my favorite. They've come to Brighton every summer for years, since before they went off to school. He studied the law, I believe. He's always been bookish." She glanced at Arielle, whose cheeks were still pink. "That wasn't a typical introduction, but I daresay he won't forget you."

"Livvie!" Arielle's color rose higher. "I don't know when I've ever been more mortified! It's bad enough to act like a goose, but to have such a witness to it!"

Olivia laughed. "I don't think Lord Patrick minded."

"He might not, but how am I ever to look him in the face?"

Olivia continued chortling until they'd reached their own correct door and passed inside.

\*\*\*

Lord Patrick Alexander had never looked forward to a public assembly with as much enthusiasm. Having come to Brighton most summers since he was old enough not to be left at Marsham Hall with a nurse, the balls at the Old Ship and the Castle had grown rather stale. They were always crowded and always attended by the same people. He couldn't deny that it was pleasant to know most of the company, unlike in London where, however large one's acquaintance, one always seemed to be among strangers. But there was little variety in the available dance partners, and half of the room was generally in love with his brother. Michael's popularity had never made Patrick jealous, nor had his inheritance of their father's title. Patrick hadn't yet met a woman who drew his eye enough to care.

Until the other morning. He didn't know what it was about Miss Arielle Farley. Ordinarily, he would have called her cute—pretty, at best—but her hair was striking: an auburn so rich it was almost wine red. Her fierce blush should have clashed with that hair, but somehow the effect was endearing, and he'd wanted to set her at ease. And those big, bright aquamarine eyes! Most Incomparables—the idealized *crème de la crème* of the *haute ton*—would die to have eyes like that.

So Patrick arrived at the Old Ship in good time, dressed with a touch more than his usual care. The Farleys hadn't arrived yet, which gave him an opportunity to casually seek out gossip about the new ward. He learned quickly that she'd only been with Lady Priscilla for a little over a week and that she'd been found washed ashore with no memories of her past or her family. This intriguing intelligence only made him more eager to know her better.

He was across the room talking to a friend when the Farleys were announced. Lady Priscilla soon moved away to join some of the older ladies with seats along the wall to gossip while watching the dancing. Arielle clung to Miss Farley's arm and stared around, wide-eyed, as if terrified to find herself here. Patrick excused himself and made his way across the room, keeping her in his sight. He'd tried a couple times since their first meeting to convince himself that he must have been mistaken in her appearance; surely, the light must have played tricks with the color of her hair and eyes. It was no trick, however. Her dress was simply cut in white jaconet, and the only color came from strings of aquamarine beads at her wrist and throat, which emphasized her eyes. More beads were pinned in her hair, and he admired the simplicity of it. She didn't need an elaborate headdress of feathers and jewels. She was no Incomparable, but she had her own stunning way about her.

Arielle saw him when he was a few yards away, and he watched her cheeks flush as she grasped Miss Farley's arm tighter.

"Miss Farley, Miss Arielle." Patrick stopped before them and bowed. "It's a pleasure to see you here tonight. Miss Arielle, may I be so bold as to solicit your hand for the first dance?"

She blinked at him, clearly alarmed.

Miss Farley shot her a wry look and grinned at Patrick. "You may, your lordship. Arielle would be honored."

Arielle managed a nod, though Patrick thought she'd rather flee the room. He proffered his arm, and she rested her silk-gloved hand on it. As he led her to the floor, he couldn't help leaning toward her and saying, "Are you afraid of dancing with me, Miss Arielle?"

"Yes," she replied candidly. She bit her lower lip. "No. I don't know. I'm still flustered that you should have seen me be so goose-witted as to go to the wrong house. I apologize again for that, by the way. Brighton probably seems like a very small town to you, but I still find it somewhat overwhelming."

"That's perfectly natural," he conceded with a smile.

"And if I'm being honest, I'll admit that I'm afraid of dancing at all. It's one thing to practice the steps in Aunt Prissy's drawing room, but another entirely to perform them in an assembly such as this."

Patrick glanced around the room. It was probably the least intimidating gathering he'd encountered in years. But for a girl so new to society, with such a sensitivity to embarrassment, it must be alarming.

"Then I'm the perfect first partner." He smiled reassuringly. "I know all the steps and can guide you through them. I have no problem with you stepping on my toes. And if a mistake *is* made, you may lay the blame fully on me. I won't mind."

This brought a slight curve to her lips. He wouldn't be so bold as to call it a smile, but almost. He could feel her relax the slightest bit.

"I hope it won't come to that," she said. "But thank you."

The first dance was a Scotch reel, and to Patrick's surprise and admiration, Arielle danced it faultlessly. About halfway through the dance, her almost-smile became genuine, and he loved to see how it lit her whole face. They were both out of breath by the time the dance ended, and Patrick was glad to have her hand back on his arm as he escorted her toward her guardian.

"You misled me, Miss Arielle," he accused teasingly. "You dance beautifully. You couldn't have been afraid of dancing—you must have said it only to spare my feelings because you were, in fact, afraid of me."

"No, no! Never. I was dreadfully afraid of dancing in public, and if there's anyone to thank for a wonderful dance, they are my partner—" she inclined her head to him, "—and Livvie, who taught me."

"I can take no credit, I assure you."

"Then I shall have to thank Livvie," Arielle said with laughter in her eyes.

Patrick was just about to ask if he could take her to get

lemonade when Michael intercepted them. His brother bowed and apologized for the interruption with the suave confidence of a duke for whom apologies were mere form.

"Patrick, will you be so good as to introduce me to your bewitching partner?" Michael never once took his eyes from Arielle.

Stifling a sigh, Patrick opened his mouth to make the introduction, realizing as he did that Arielle had gone still. Her extraordinary eyes were fixed on the Duke of Marsham, and she looked so stunned she could be knocked over with a feather. Patrick felt a sinking in his gut, a familiar pang as yet another young woman fell instantly under his brother's spell. He schooled his features into a calm mask. Michael was handsome, rich, and titled. He was a Corinthian, a true out-and-outer. Everyone fell at his feet, men and women alike. Scores of women set their caps at him each season. Patrick, too, admired his eldest brother, and he didn't begrudge him any young woman in the world…. Except, it turned out, Arielle Farley.

# Chapter 6

Arielle didn't mean to stare. She knew it was rude and indelicate, but she simply couldn't tear her gaze away. The gentleman standing in front of them was dressed to the nines in a black tailcoat and white knee breeches. He was tall and well-muscled, with chiseled features, dark hair, and deep, dark eyes.

She knew those eyes, that face. This was the man she'd been hoping to meet. The one she remembered. Almost. She didn't remember who he was or how she knew him, but her stomach swooped in the oddest way, as if she were falling, and she remembered that she loved him. Or she thought she did. It was all so muddled and unclear, so she stared.

Lord Patrick introduced him as his eldest brother, the Duke of Marsham. Arielle registered in the back of her mind that Lord Patrick's voice had lost the teasing laughter of a moment ago; it was curiously flat and dull. A glance showed her that his face, too, had gone expressionless. But before she could wonder at this, the Duke begged the honor of dancing the next set with her. Her heart leapt. Not only had she been introduced to the man she'd been looking for, she would get to dance with him. She had accepted and traded gentlemen before her mind caught up with her. She gathered her wits enough to thank

Lord Patrick for the dance, leaving him with a shy smile.

The set was forming as Marsham led her to it. Arielle recognized the circle as the beginning of La Boulanger, and she took her place beside the duke at the top, as he was the only duke currently in residence and therefore the most prestigious person in the room. This gave her a momentary wave of fear—she would surely embarrass herself *and* His Grace if she were in the first couple. But as she turned her nervous gaze on him, she found Marsham watching her, a smile at the corner of his mouth. She blushed and smiled and forgot to worry as the dance began. Sidelong glances were all she could contrive as they danced around the circle, but when they took hands and turned together, their gazes locked. Their eyes were like magnets, finding each other again whenever they were separated by turning with the other dancers. Other couples were talking together, but Arielle and the duke didn't speak a word.

When the dance ended, Marsham asked if Arielle would like lemonade. She accepted, and they moved together to the refreshments. Arielle took a glass of the cool liquid and was about to drink when a bright voice called her name. Letitia Goulding approached the table, looking as lovely as an angel in her white crepe.

Marsham obligingly stepped back so that the friends could greet each other with a kiss to the cheek. "You two know each other?" he asked, smiling.

"Oh, yes!" Letitia gushed. "We've been friends all this week, haven't we, Arielle? And have you borrowed *Udolpho* yet?"

Arielle opened her mouth to answer, but the duke protested. "No books in a ballroom, ladies, I beg you. Even by the splendid Mrs. Radcliffe."

Letitia laughed. "Perhaps, Arielle, I'll have to sneak you away to a corner later when you have no partner to complain." She gave Marsham an arch look.

"I don't think Miss Arielle will want for partners," he declared.

Arielle blushed. "I would think, rather, that Miss Goulding won't have the opportunity to sneak away."

"She certainly won't right now," Marsham said. "Will you do me the honor of the next set, Miss Goulding?"

Letitia accepted, and Arielle took a sip of her lemonade. They chatted for a few moments more, then Arielle excused herself to join Olivia, who was standing nearby. Letitia took her place on Marsham's arm and said, "Tomorrow, then, Arielle, I'll call on you and we'll take a good long walk to discuss books. No one can argue *that*."

Standing beside Olivia, who was conversing amiably with the young widow on her other side, Arielle finished her lemonade. She was surprised when the owner of the Old Ship, who was serving as master of ceremonies for the evening, approached, bowed, and asked for the privilege of introducing a young gentleman who particularly wanted to be acquainted with her. He was a Mr. Sharpton—nearly as tall as the duke and thin as a rail, with a pointed nose and heavy eyebrows. He bowed and asked for the next dance. Arielle peeked at Olivia, who made no protest. She accepted, and when the next set formed, she and Mr. Sharpton were in it. He was a fair dancer, and she enjoyed herself, though he showed an inclination for talking throughout, which didn't suit her. Arielle supposed that if one wanted to get to know one's partner, talking during the dance was the surest way, but she still wasn't confident enough in her own ability to do both. So her answers were short, and she only half paid attention to Mr. Sharpton. But he didn't seem to notice, and left her after the dance with an assurance that he'd gladly stand up with her again.

She was spared the necessity of responding by Olivia, who brought another gentleman forward for introduction. He asked for a dance later in the evening, which she willingly granted.

"The next is a quadrille," Olivia whispered in her ear. "And after that comes a waltz."

"Thank goodness. I'm perfectly happy to stand quietly with you for a while."

Olivia grinned. "Your popularity was ensured as soon as the Duke of Marsham danced with you, particularly when everyone could see how pleased he was with his partner."

"You should have warned me," Arielle said, pretending to be stern. "Perhaps I didn't want to be popular."

"And if I had, would you have refused to dance with him?" Olivia raised her eyebrows. Arielle blushed. "I thought not."

Arielle bit her lip, but a small giggle escaped. She and Olivia turned to watch the dancers. Letitia Goulding was dancing again, and she moved with such grace that Arielle was almost envious of her new friend.

"She's so perfect that I want to be jealous," she murmured to Olivia. "But it's impossible to hate her."

"I'm sure she has her faults like everyone else. But I'd rather you like her anyway. It's better to like people than to envy them."

The two of them were so caught up in trying to memorize the steps of the quadrille that they didn't notice Lord Patrick Alexander standing beside them until he spoke.

"Miss Arielle, may I have the next, or are you already spoken for?"

Arielle jumped. "I'm afraid the next is impossible, Lord Patrick," she said. From his crestfallen look, she thought he must assume that she was promised to dance with someone else. She explained, "The next is a waltz."

His brows pressed together slightly. "Does Lady Priscilla forbid you to waltz?"

"No, not at all." Arielle glanced at Olivia, who had suddenly fallen into deep conversation with the neighboring widow again. "It's only that I don't know how. The quadrille and the waltz were not done when Livvie came out, so she couldn't teach me those. She hired a dance master, but he isn't available for two weeks, so until then I'm sitting out."

"That won't do," he said. "You're already the most talked about young lady in Brighton, and your popularity is rising to the level of Miss Goulding. If you sit out every quadrille and waltz, your remaining dances will be bespoken so quickly that I'll never get another chance."

He said this with a hint of that teasing smile again. Arielle much preferred this to the flat, expressionless politeness he'd shown while introducing her to his brother. It wasn't hard now to see the family resemblance, though he was shorter and less athletically built than Marsham. His hair was lighter, his features softer, and his whole demeanor quieter and less prepossessing.

There was a pause between songs as partners changed.

"If you ask nicely, I could save you one."

This made his smile twitch wider. "Or I could do you one better: what if I were to teach you?"

"I beg your pardon?"

"I know both the waltz and the quadrille. Rather than waiting weeks for a dancing master, I'm offering my services."

"You don't know what you're offering. I'm a slow learner."

"I'm patient."

"Be serious," Arielle protested as the opening strains of the waltz began. "You can't want to give dance lessons. You must have countless better things to do."

"On the contrary, my time in Brighton is entirely at my disposal. I won't take up as a dancing master, but I think I should enjoy teaching you immensely."

Arielle wasn't sure what to make of that pronouncement. She returned her attention to the dancers, who were paired off, each couple unexpectedly close together. The dance began, and the couples moved and spun as if each had fused together, becoming one unit rather than two separate dancers. She saw the Duke of Marsham dancing with a lady she didn't know, and she suddenly had a very strong desire to learn to waltz so that *she* could be the woman he held so close.

She shot a sidelong glance at Lord Patrick. His gray eyes twinkled, but she thought he looked sincere. "I accept, but only if you teach Livvie too. She'd like it of all things."

"It would be my pleasure."

With his offer accepted, Arielle expected Lord Patrick to go find another partner. She wasn't the only young lady standing with the chaperones. He seemed content instead to stand beside her and point out aspects of the dance to her notice. Two other young men solicited her hand for the waltz within the first few minutes, but she politely declined, and Lord Patrick cheerfully kept his place, despite the dark looks thrown at him by the slighted applicants.

When the waltz ended, it was time to go in to dinner, and Lord Patrick graciously offered to escort Arielle and her guardians. Arielle couldn't help noticing a few more dark looks aimed at the duke's brother, and Marsham himself raised an eyebrow at Lord Patrick as he passed with Miss Goulding on his arm. She looked up at her escort curiously.

"Are you doing something shocking by escorting us in to dinner?" she asked. "Only it seems all the gentlemen think you are."

Lord Patrick's eyes twinkled. "I've raised a good deal of jealousy by accompanying the loveliest girl in the room."

"Oh, stuff," she said dismissively. "If you're resorting to flattery rather than telling me the truth, I'll say nothing more."

"Miss Arielle, I have not lied to you, nor will I," he replied, quite serious now. "Perhaps my brother is due an equal share of jealousy for accompanying Miss Goulding, but he's a duke."

"And as a duke, he's entitled to escort the prettiest girl?"

He shrugged.

"I think it's all a hum," she said after a moment's consideration. "Why should beauty and rank go together? And who is to determine the gradations of beauty? It's utter nonsense."

"It is, but the *beau monde* is built on nonsense. Without nonsense, society as we know it would cease to exist."

Arielle shot him a look and saw that the corner of his mouth was twitching as he tried to keep from smiling. She couldn't stop her own lips from answering that smile. "You're impossible."

"Probably," he agreed, guiding her to a chair with space for Olivia and Lady Priscilla beside her.

Impossible or not, he was true to his word, and before the evening was over he'd settled with Olivia that he would call on them during the course of Saturday morning for a dance lesson.

# Chapter 7

Letitia Goulding was as good as her word as well. She arrived late the next morning, having accompanied her mother on a call nearby and begged to be allowed to walk with Arielle. So the two stepped out, meandering along Marine Parade and up the Steine.

"Are you quite recovered from last night?" Letitia asked, taking Arielle's arm. "It was your first ball, wasn't it? I remember being so dreadfully tired after my first."

Arielle agreed. "I'm glad we're not in a rush. I don't think I can walk any faster than this." She made a face. "When I got up, I was afraid my feet wouldn't bear me at all."

"It will get better," Letitia said bracingly. "And you can take comfort in knowing you were a brilliant success."

Arielle still wasn't entirely sure what being a success at a ball meant, but Letitia seemed convinced that she was, and that it was a good thing. She accepted this and turned the subject to books, and they talked happily about Emily and Valancourt and how lovely it would be to visit southern France… but perhaps not any Gothic Italian castles.

They turned to walk back toward the beach and were hailed by the Duke of Marsham, who was just coming out of a street nearby.

"Where are you ladies off to?" he asked.

"Nowhere in particular," Letitia said brightly. "We're merely walking and discussing books. We were just turning to walk back to Lady Priscilla's house on Marine Parade."

"Then I pray you let me accompany you," he said with a bow. "I myself am intending to call on my brother who lives in that direction."

Arielle couldn't help the blush that rose at the recollection of how she had discovered Lord Patrick's house. Neither of the others noticed, however, and soon they'd rearranged themselves so that each lady had accepted one of Marsham's arms and they were strolling along together.

They fell to talking about Brighton and all the things Arielle had not yet seen: the races, the downs, the cliff walks, the castles.

"Castles?" Arielle said, unable to keep the hope from her voice.

"There must be half a dozen within a day of Brighton," confirmed the duke. "But Lewes Castle is the closest."

"It's close enough for an afternoon outing," Letitia said. "Mother and I went last year. And there's an old priory, too, if you like stone ruins."

"We should plan a day trip to visit," Marsham declared. "I'll gather a group of friends and make an event of it."

Arielle couldn't imagine anything more agreeable, though when Marsham turned those deep brown eyes on her and smiled, he could have made scrubbing floors sound appealing.

As they came up to it, Letitia pointed out the house she and her mother had hired for the season, since Arielle hadn't been there yet. It had a pleasant view of the green, but Arielle preferred Lady Priscilla's house, with the constant ambient ocean sounds.

"Miss Goulding, are you intending to walk home alone after leaving Miss Arielle in Marine Parade? That's not quite the thing." The duke's tone was light and playful, so his chiding had no bite.

"Mama was paying a call in that direction." Letitia shrugged. "I guess I hadn't thought whether she'd still be there."

"Why don't we walk you to your door to make sure you're safe? I'll escort Miss Arielle the rest of the way home, as I'm going that way already."

Letitia shrugged and agreed, kissing Arielle on the cheek before skipping up the steps of the house. She turned at the door. "Don't forget, Your Grace—you promised a castle outing, and we'll hold you to it."

"I wouldn't dream of forgetting anything that would give you ladies pleasure." He bowed gallantly. Arielle smothered a grin. Letitia giggled and disappeared inside.

Arielle and the duke talked of inconsequential things as they continued on their way, but even the weather was interesting when Marsham discussed it, smiling down at her. Arielle couldn't sneak glances around the brim of her bonnet easily, and staring up at him would have given her a crick in the neck. So she was free to notice the interested glances of the people they passed. The attention made her uncomfortable, and she might have wondered if walking with a duke was worth the gawking, except that each time she looked up into Marsham's face and saw the warmth of his eyes and smile, she forgot the rest.

Marsham left her at her door, and Arielle entered to find Mrs. Goulding in the drawing room with Aunt Prissy and Olivia.

"Ari! You're back!" Olivia beckoned her over to the seat beside her. "Did you walk home alone? Where did you leave Miss Goulding?"

"His Grace walked me home." Arielle sat, blushing. "He was coming this direction to see his brother. We didn't know you would be here, ma'am, so we walked Letitia home first."

Mrs. Goulding pressed her lips together tightly, as though she'd just eaten a sour grape.

"Then it seems I am wanted at home," she said coolly. "Please excuse me, your ladyship, Miss Farley." She rose and left.

Arielle looked after her, mystified.

\*\*\*

Arielle spent the rest of the day in the parlor with her book on her lap, but most of the time she was thinking rather than reading. No matter how she turned it over, she couldn't make sense of Mrs. Goulding's reaction. She didn't waste much time in contemplating her friend's mother. Marsham made a much pleasanter subject for thought. She reflected on the sense of falling she'd had when she met him, and how he seemed impossible to look away from. Even chatting with him about nothing had been the best half hour of her day.

"Is this what love feels like?" she murmured to the book in her hands, as if Emily St. Aubert could answer her from its pages. "Is he the one I'm supposed to marry?"

She'd gained no further insight into the consequences of not marrying her true love by the end of a year and a day. No more memories had surfaced at all. But there was still time, and she had no satisfying conclusions to offer herself, so she determined to wait and see what her next meeting with the

## CHAPTER 7

duke would bring and resolved to put him from her mind until then.

The next morning, Lord Patrick called at the very beginning of acceptable visiting hours. He was shown to the drawing room, and by the time Arielle entered with Olivia, he'd moved most of the furniture back against the wall. He straightened up from the chair he was shoving and bowed.

"I do hope you still want a dance lesson," he said, "because I've already taken the liberty of preparing the room."

Olivia assured him that they did. "Aunt Prissy will be here soon to play for us, but we thought it might be best to learn the steps without music first."

"Quite right," he said. "I thought we might begin with the quadrille, but we'll need a fourth person. I didn't think I had a right to invite anyone else along to a private lesson."

Olivia pondered for a second. "I think James will do." She pulled the cord and James appeared momentarily. The footman was a friendly fellow in his forties, and no stranger to the Farleys' strange whims. He didn't bat an eye at the request that he learn the quadrille with them, merely bowed and declared himself at their service.

"You'll dance with me," Olivia told him. "If we don't get it quite right, well, no harm done."

"What do you mean, Livvie? Of course you'll get it right," Arielle said.

"I only mean that spinsters my age don't get asked to dance at balls." Olivia shrugged. "I believe I was asked once last year, by Mr. Porter."

Arielle opened her mouth to protest, but Olivia cut her off. "Let's not waste Lord Patrick's time. Do, please, show us the quadrille, your lordship."

Arielle's cheeks heated, suddenly realizing that spinster status was probably a sore point for Olivia, and it wasn't something to be blabbered about in front of a guest and a servant. She obediently got into position where Lord Patrick showed her. The steps to the dance were not difficult, as they were similar to most of the country dances, but remembering what order they came in and what direction to skip was. There were several near misses, and Arielle stepped on Lord Patrick's toe once—her silk slippers did no damage, and she was glad it wasn't his Hessians landing on *her* toe—before they took a break. Aunt Prissy had come in unnoticed, and now she offered her services at the pianoforte. The steps weren't much easier with music, but it did at least keep them all in time together.

After an hour, they were able to make it through the dance without material fault. Olivia dismissed James from the room, as they wouldn't need him for the waltz, but she charged him first to send up lemonade. Drinks arrived, and they all rested and sipped the cool beverage. Arielle stood by the window and turned her chilled glass in her hands, running the steps of the quadrille through her mind to keep from getting nervous about learning the waltz. She'd watched it at the Old Ship, and it had been a beautiful, graceful dance. But it involved standing awfully close to a gentleman with his hand on her waist, and it offered more than the usual opportunities for stepping on one's partner's toes.

Lord Patrick set down his glass. "Shall we waltz?"

Olivia got to her feet, and Arielle set down her own glass. "Livvie first," she said. "I'd like to watch before I try."

"We're not at that point yet. I'll teach you both the steps together. Come here to the middle of the room."

They began by learning what he called a box step, stepping

back with the right foot, to the side with the left, and then together with the right. Then the opposite: front with the left, side to the right, together. They repeated these steps over and over. Lord Patrick showed them how the first of the three beats was heavier, with the full foot on the ground, and the other two were lighter, up on the toes. Arielle's head was spinning with down-up-up and back-side-together. She suddenly felt like she had three feet too many, and they were all getting tangled. She bit her lip and tried to swallow her frustration. Adding in the music from Aunt Prissy, even slowly, only made it worse.

When Lord Patrick decided they were ready to try with a partner—how he could think that, Arielle didn't know, because *she*, at least, hadn't shown any improvement in the last half hour—he took Olivia's hands and showed them how the gentleman steps with the opposite foot: as the lady steps back, the gentleman steps forward. They did the steps together, and even Olivia got mixed up as she watched his lordship's feet doing the opposite of hers.

When it was Arielle's turn to try with Lord Patrick, she kept her eyes fixed on her feet. She could feel him watching her, but she was too embarrassed to look up.

"I'm sorry I'm such a slow learner," she muttered after stepping wrong again.

"Don't be." His voice was quiet and gentle, without any teasing. "I told you I'm patient."

He called for a break then. Arielle resisted the urge to flop haphazardly onto the couch by the wall, as well as the stronger urge to go hide in her bedroom with a book. Lord Patrick was being very kind to teach them, and she owed him respect. She settled for sitting primly on her chair and taking slow, calming breaths, while listening to the conversation on the other side of the room.

"My brother has taken it into his head to get up an expedition to Lewes," Lord Patrick was saying. "A regular exploring party to see the castle and the ruined priory, with lunch at the inn. Will you all come with us? Miss Arielle hasn't seen anything of the country yet, has she?"

"Oh, what a lovely idea!" Aunt Prissy gushed, her face crinkling into her brightest smile. "I've always loved seeing old ruins. They're so poetic, you know. Ari, dear, isn't it a splendid plan?"

Arielle nodded, declining to mention that she had been present when the notion had first come up. "I should very much like to see them."

"Then it's settled. Only let us know when it is to happen, and we'll be glad to come."

"Next Saturday, if the weather is fine. Would you allow me to drive you? I know you don't keep a carriage of your own."

Many families in Brighton didn't keep a carriage, as the village was small enough to walk everywhere. But Lewes was too far to walk, and Lady Priscilla accepted Lord Patrick's offer with good grace.

Before long, it was time to dance again. Arielle's improvement was slow but real, and after another half hour, she managed to dance while holding Lord Patrick's hands without mistake. Aunt Prissy was still playing much more slowly than the proper tempo. Before having her speed it up, however, they changed positions. Lord Patrick put one hand at Arielle's waist while she lifted her skirt a few inches, and he took her free hand with his. Arielle's face flamed brighter than ever, and she couldn't meet his eyes. She fixed her gaze on his cravat and counted out the steps, frowning in concentration.

"Don't think so hard," he murmured. "Listen to the music."

Arielle tried, but his closeness flustered her. He seemed disappointed when he finally called a halt and stepped back. He had lived up to his promise of patience, but it couldn't have been easy. She hung her head and wouldn't look at him.

"I'll call again on Tuesday, if you don't mind." He addressed Olivia, who thanked him for his generosity. "Practice in the meantime."

When he was gone, Arielle did what she'd been wanting for the past two hours and fled to her room to read undisturbed. By dinner time, she was calm again. Aunt Prissy informed her that James had turned away three gentleman callers while they were dancing.

"They were all quite taken by you at the ball."

None of the callers had been the Duke of Marsham, so Arielle wasn't disappointed to have missed them. She couldn't decide which was a more awkward way to spend a morning: failing a dance lesson or sitting for a half hour or more with unfamiliar gentlemen. It was a moot point. She'd already tried one; there were plenty of days ahead when she could expect to try the other.

Olivia insisted on dancing again after dinner, practicing the steps of the waltz over and over at various tempos until even Arielle could do them consistently. Afterward, the three of them repaired to the parlor, where Arielle read to the others while they embroidered. Aunt Prissy insisted that someday she'd teach Arielle how to sew, as it was a useful skill, but for now they were all enjoying Mrs. Radcliffe's tale.

# Chapter 8

On Sunday evening, Patrick walked to the Steine for the weekly promenade, but he found little interest in it. He didn't see the Farleys, but he saw his brother flirting with Miss Goulding and another young lady whose name he didn't know. Some friends invited him to play cards, but he knew they'd be playing high, and he had too little fortune as a youngest son to risk gambling it all away. He left early and spent some time walking along the beach. The sky glowed primrose and amber, reflecting in the water and on the wet stones of the beach. Eventually he turned, and he came back along Marine Parade, passing Lady Priscilla Farley's house as he came. Through an open window, he could hear the strains of a quadrille played on the pianoforte. Shrieks of giddy laughter met his ears, and he stopped on the street, arrested by the sound. They were obviously having great fun together. He couldn't remember when his family had laughed together like that—not since Frederick had gone away to school, leaving him the only son at home, certainly. Even then, it had only been the boys, never their parents. But he thought he could pick out Lady Priscilla's laugh amid the commotion inside. He thought wistfully that he'd like to be in such a lighthearted family, and he wished that he could join theirs for more than a morning.

"Wrong way, Livvie!" Arielle's voice carried out to him, followed by a squeal and a giggle.

He couldn't help smiling at the brightness of Arielle's laugh. But it was impossible not to contrast it to how solemn and tense she'd been during their lesson. Had she been somber solely because of her struggle to learn? Or had she been quiet because he was there? He sighed. Both, more than likely. But as he walked on, their laughter still ringing out into the street, he knew that he would do anything to make her more comfortable, comfortable enough that she could laugh like that with him.

When Patrick called again on Tuesday, he found Mr. Sharpton already seated in the Farleys' drawing room. Lady Priscilla rose and greeted him, and Patrick bowed over both Olivia's and Arielle's hands as well before seating himself across the room from the gentleman. Sharpton was one of Michael's set, but Patrick had never much liked him. Sharpton cared only about horses, hounds, and prizefights, and he was a rattle. Just now he was going on about his house in the country and the woods and fields roundabout where he'd had so many successful hunts.

Patrick watched Arielle, at whom Sharpton's boasts were aimed. She smiled politely, nodding when called for, but she lacked the lively spark he'd seen at the ball. The poor girl was bored stiff. Patrick wished he could engage her in conversation instead, but interrupting would have been indecorous, and besides, he wasn't seated near enough. He contented himself with catching her eye when she glanced at him and winking. The look she sent back was so expressive a plea for rescue that he jumped into the next available opening in Sharpton's discourse.

"Did you know, Sharpton, that my brother is going to Lewes to look at horses today? It seems one of his team is not up to snuff, and he got word about a pair of grays for sale."

"In Lewes?" Sharpton protested, his heavy eyebrows lowering forbiddingly. "Not a good horse to be had in the whole county. He ought to go to Tattersall's. London's not so very far, not if you want a decent piece of horseflesh."

"He wouldn't listen to my opinion." Patrick shrugged. "He declared he didn't have time to be driving back and forth to town. Maybe he'd listen to you, though. He was fixing to leave this morning, I believe."

Sharpton rose abruptly and bowed to the ladies. "Forgive me, ladies, but a man can't in good conscience allow a friend to purchase a bad horse. It simply won't do."

"Perfectly right," Arielle agreed. "It was lovely to see you, of course, but don't let us detain you from your mission."

A moment later, Sharpton was gone.

When they heard the front door close behind him, Arielle let out her breath. "Thank you, Lord Patrick. Your rescue was most timely."

"Ari," Miss Farley warned. Arielle blushed and lowered her eyes to her lap. A proper young lady probably oughtn't reveal her distaste for one suitor in the presence of another.

"He *was* dull," Lady Priscilla admitted candidly. "And it was very well done, Lord Patrick. But I do hope that wasn't a lie."

"Not a bit. Michael was indeed planning to drive to Lewes today. The pair of horses in question actually came recommended highly by a trusted source." He felt a smile pulling at his lips, proud that he'd been the hero Arielle needed at the moment. "How long had he been sitting with you?"

"Nearly an hour." Arielle's eyes darted to his and told him

just how long that time had felt.

"Well." Olivia stood, and Patrick could see she was smiling, however hard she tried to hide it. "Would you like tea, Lord Patrick, or shall we get right to the lesson?" She crossed the room and poked her head out, instructing whoever was there that no more visitors were to be allowed in.

"Let's see what you remember." Patrick stood and began moving furniture. Arielle joined in with a will, and Lady Priscilla moved to the piano stool. "Waltz first."

Lady Priscilla started to play, and both Miss Farley and Arielle demonstrated that they remembered the steps when dancing them alone. Patrick stepped forward and danced with Miss Farley for a moment, pleased with her progress, then turned to Arielle. She seemed more relaxed today, perhaps because she'd had time to practice, perhaps because he'd just gotten rid of a very tedious suitor. They took their position, and she danced without misstep.

Miss Farley applauded when he called for a pause. "You've gotten it, Ari!"

Arielle blushed and smiled shyly.

"Now to bring it to ballroom level," Patrick said. His mouth twitched at the look of alarm that crossed the girl's face, but he kept his smile hidden so as not to offend her, and he spoke gently. "The music will be faster at a ball, and your partner will guide you around the room. The steps are the same, but instead of making a square, you will follow your partner's lead."

Arielle's eyes were wide, but she nodded.

"Don't worry, Miss Arielle," he murmured as Lady Priscilla began the first few bars of the waltz again. "Don't think. Just follow my lead."

He danced her around the room. At first she was so stiff

in his arms that her movements were jerky, but gradually she relaxed again, and the dance flowed smoothly. On the third time around the room, he led her through a turn, then a more complex one. She stumbled once, but recovered quickly. Lady Priscilla brought the song to a close.

Patrick stepped back and dropped his hands, though he wouldn't have minded staying close to her. She was half panting for breath and half laughing, and she sank into a chair.

"If that's what a waltz is supposed to be, it might be my favorite dance. It was like flying."

Patrick silently agreed: if he could waltz with Arielle, it was his favorite dance by far.

***

Patrick was late to that week's ball at the Old Ship. He strode through the door, kicking himself. Not only had he missed the chance to be Arielle's first partner, by now her dance card was probably full. He had every intention of seeking her out immediately and claiming whatever dance she had left. But Lady Caroline Hervey stopped him as he passed her chair and asked after his mother and whether she'd be joining them in Brighton this year. Having just received a letter from the dowager duchess, he could tell her that his mother planned to join them in another week or two when she was confident that Frederick's wife was well cared for in her newly interesting condition. Lady Caroline had a good many questions to add, and Patrick smothered a sigh as he answered them all. She was a dear friend of his mother's, after all, and it wouldn't pay to be rude. But when a waltz struck up, his attention was drawn away to the dance floor. He looked for Arielle, hoping foolishly but fervently that she somehow wouldn't have a partner yet.

His eye, however, was caught by her vibrant hair as she took her place with…

Michael.

Patrick's stomach dropped to his knees. He'd spent hours teaching Arielle, only for his brother to share her first public waltz. It was his own fault, he knew. He should have bespoken the dance on Tuesday when he'd had the opportunity. But knowing who to blame didn't make it any easier to watch the two of them smiling at each other as if there were no one else in the room. Arielle looked so relaxed in his arms, gliding through the steps effortlessly. As if she'd only needed the right partner to unlock her gift.

Lady Caroline said something that recalled Patrick to where he was. Instead of answering her question, however, he excused himself. He turned on his heel to leave the ballroom, unwilling to watch a minute longer, but he paused at the sight of Miss Farley at the edge of the floor, swaying to the music. He would have no pleasure from this assembly, but perhaps someone else could.

Miss Farley looked up at Patrick in surprise when he addressed her, and her mouth positively fell open when he asked her to dance.

"I didn't teach you so that you could stand and watch," he said, flashing a smile that was almost real.

"I really thought you did." Miss Farley took his arm. "I thought…." She glanced at Arielle dancing with Michael. She left the thought unfinished and said lightly, "Why don't we show everyone what a good teacher you are?"

Miss Farley was an excellent dancer, and she smiled in delight as they twirled through the room. She laughed in surprise as he executed a sudden, tricky turn. The sound drew Arielle's gaze from halfway across the floor. Arielle's face lit up at the sight of her friend dancing, and she spared Patrick a warm look of gratitude.

His heart did a little somersault. For a moment, he didn't begrudge Michael the dance with Arielle, because it had left Patrick free to engage in mild heroism.

When the dance ended, Patrick and Miss Farley moved toward Arielle. They saw Michael raise Arielle's hand to his lips. She blushed, said something quietly, then turned to greet Miss Farley with outstretched hands.

"You were right, Ari," Miss Farley said, her face still glowing. "Waltzing like that is just like flying."

Arielle beamed at her before turning her big, aquamarine eyes on Patrick. "Thank you, my lord, for teaching us both."

Patrick bowed. "It was my pleasure, Miss Arielle. I know I'm late in the asking, but have you any dances unpromised?"

"One." She exchanged an amused look with Miss Farley. "The quadrille."

He looked between them, wondering at their secret joke, but Lord Preston appeared then to claim Arielle's hand for the next dance. Patrick escorted Miss Farley from the floor and stood back along the wall to wait for the quadrille.

After a few minutes, Michael took a place at his side. He surveyed the dance, then said quietly, "That was a clever tactic, using Miss Farley to ingratiate yourself with Miss Arielle."

"It wasn't a tactic." Patrick looked sidelong at his brother. "I know that Miss Farley enjoys dancing but she rarely gets the chance."

"Well, Miss Arielle noticed." Michael met Patrick's eye, nodded, and disappeared back into the crowd.

## CHAPTER 8

Patrick watched him go. He tried to suppress the burst of triumph that surged through him. It was rare for Michael to acknowledge that Patrick had scored a point.

The duke was only four years his elder, but their dispositions were dissimilar enough to have given them little in common all their lives. Patrick was quiet and bookish, though he was passably capable in most sporting endeavors. Michael was much more athletic, driven to be the best at every sport, besides being more outgoing and social. His parties in town were the stuff of legend, and he never wanted for female companionship. If it came to a contest for a woman's heart, Patrick had no illusions: his brother would always win.

But he also knew that Michael's favorites never lasted long before he was on to the next girl, the next flirtation. Despite their mother's often-professed wishes, Michael showed no signs of settling down. He would flirt with Arielle, attach her, raise her hopes, and then drop her completely when he left Brighton, if not before. She would be a passing fancy, and she would end brokenhearted.

Patrick wouldn't stand idly by and watch that happen to Arielle.

# Chapter 9

Saturday dawned sunny and warm, and not a cloud in sight: the ideal day for an excursion to Lewes Castle. Lord Patrick pulled up in front of the house at ten o'clock. Olivia had been watching out the front window while Lindsay put the finishing touches on Arielle's hair. In moments, they tied on bonnets and pulled on gloves and silk shawls.

Arielle eyed the restlessly stamping horses with trepidation. She was certain that she'd spent no time with horses in the same way that she knew Hessy was the first cat she'd met. But she'd made friends with Hessy quickly—he now slept curled up beside her in bed every night—and perhaps she could befriend the horses too. She approached their heads cautiously, reassured that a groom held their reins and they couldn't harm her. The nearest horse peered at her through one liquid chocolate eye rimmed with the longest lashes. She smiled, her fear fading in the face of admiration. These horses were beautiful, majestic, noble. She slowly reached to run one hand down the horse's long face. It stilled, not taking its eyes from hers, calming so completely that one would never know it had been restless.

"I didn't know you liked horses." Lord Patrick's voice from behind startled her, but she didn't move from where she was.

## CHAPTER 9

"Neither did I," she murmured. "But how could anyone not?"

The horse blew softly as if in agreement. Arielle smiled and stroked its cheek.

"I think Pevensey likes you too." Lord Patrick patted the horse's shoulder. "I'm sure his brother Hastings would appreciate your attention as well, but we really ought to be getting on the road."

"Right." Arielle gave the huge chestnut horse—Pevensey—another pat. "Sorry." She allowed Lord Patrick to hand her into the open landau with the Farleys.

After making sure they were comfortable, he climbed up to the bench and took the reins. They were to meet the Duke of Marsham and a few others at his house on the Steine before taking the road northeast to Lewes. They didn't talk much as they drove through town. Arielle was too excited, and the rattle of the wheels was loud on the cobbles.

When they arrived, the last of the carriages were pulling up: four in all, with Marsham driving the Gouldings. Mr. Sharpton and Lord Preston each drove their own gig, and there were three ladies with them. With a cheer, the company rolled out. The broad green sweep of the downs opened before them as they left Brighton—flat fields and low rolling hills that were almost a verdant ocean, to Arielle's amazement.

They'd been driving a few minutes when Lord Patrick called back over his shoulder. "I didn't get a chance to ask on Thursday—what was so funny about the quadrille? I know you were laughing at a private joke when I asked you for the dance."

Olivia turned pink and gave a nervous laugh. Arielle grinned.

"Practicing the quadrille didn't go especially smoothly," she explained, leaning forward. "James joined us, of course, but we were short a fourth, so we had to enlist Lindsay, who'd never learned the steps. And then Livvie decided that she ought to take the place as my partner, but that only confused things more because she had to do everything backward." Olivia's cheeks turned brighter. "I don't think a single one of us made it out of that practice without a scar."

Lord Patrick glanced back at her, a spark in his eye to answer hers. "Do I guess rightly in thinking the practice devolved into giggles and an utter inability to put two steps together?"

"Quite right," Arielle agreed. "After that we had to pretend to have a fourth, because Lindsay would have none of it, and I wouldn't dance with Livvie as my partner again."

Olivia made a face at Arielle behind Lord Patrick's back. "And yet, you learned to dance."

"She did indeed." Lord Patrick cast a glance back at Olivia now. "I would never have known that such disastrous practices had led to her performance in the ballroom if the two of you hadn't given it away."

Arielle was surprised by how soon they reached Lewes. She'd been so caught up in chatting about this and that and enjoying the breeze in her face that the time seemed to vanish. Soon, however, they were pulling up before the castle. The enormous stone structure capped a low hill, rising as if the stonework were part of the earth itself.

"The castle was built by William de Warrenne in the eleventh century," Lord Patrick told them, pulling to a stop a short distance from his brother's gig. "He was the son-in-law of William the Conqueror. He was made the Earl of Surrey and held the manors surrounding Brighton."

It was kind of Lord Patrick to share that information, but it meant nothing to Arielle. She had no idea who those people were. The castle was several hundred years old; that was information enough for the moment. She smiled at Lord Patrick as he handed them down and looked around as everyone else disembarked from the other carriages.

Letitia beamed as she found Arielle. "Isn't it something?" she asked, waving at the castle. "It's not French or Italian, and I'm sure there are no great mysteries in it, but it's still so grand."

"Very," Arielle agreed.

"Let's walk a bit and get a better look."

Letitia linked her arm through Arielle's and started up the hill toward the castle. The others fell in with them. Aunt Prissy, Olivia, and Mrs. Goulding walked behind, along with Mrs. Ingersoll, a widow who had come with her younger sister, Miss Rowles. Miss Rowles walked arm in arm with Miss Crewe, and the gentlemen strode along beside them, making themselves agreeable to everyone. Or rather, to Arielle's mind, Mr. Sharpton talked more than was desirable, and Lord Patrick didn't say much at all. But the Duke of Marsham stayed close to Arielle and Letitia, and he couldn't fail to be agreeable.

They spent the next hour walking the grounds and exploring what was available of the castle to be seen. The party broke up into smaller groups. Arielle and Letitia continued to be attended by His Grace. When Aunt Prissy grew tired, Lord Patrick found a shady place for the chaperones to rest and wait for the others. Arielle noticed this and was touched by his thoughtfulness.

As they meandered around the grassy hilltop, Arielle couldn't help but think that the view of the town must be even better from atop the castle walls. The longer they explored, the more she wanted to find out how far across the downs she could see. So when they fell in with the other young people and Letitia set to telling them all an amusing anecdote from one of her visits to Almack's in town, Arielle slipped away. She'd seen a set of stairs that led to the battlements, and she climbed them eagerly.

The view was no less spectacular than she'd imagined. She could see for miles: Lewes spread below her looking tiny and quaint amid a great sea of green downs. The sun's warm glow made every color vivid and alive. Arielle could hear Letitia still telling her story and the laughs of the group. She smiled to herself at her friend's lively and engaging manner, but she was happy to have this moment apart. From where she stood, she couldn't see the young people, nor the chaperones, and she allowed herself to feel alone in the great big world. She closed her eyes and tipped her face to the sun, breathing the fresh, wide open air.

A strong hand gripped her upper arm, and her eyes snapped open. She stepped on the hem of her dress and lost her balance, wobbling perilously close to the edge. Arielle stifled a shriek as the hand hauled her backward until she stumbled against a man's broad chest, his other hand coming to her waist to steady her.

"Forgive me, Miss Arielle," Marsham murmured from over her shoulder. "I would have spoken sooner, but I was afraid that if I startled you, you'd fall. I preferred to wait until I was close enough to catch you."

His deep voice in her ear and the warmth of his body behind her sent a tremor through her that had nothing to do with a fear of tumbling from the battlements. She pressed a hand against her racing heart. "Your care was justified," she said, craning her neck to look up at him past her bonnet. "Thank you."

## CHAPTER 9

"Seeing you that close to the edge frightened me, I must admit—and I don't scare easily." The stark concern on his face softened into a smile. He loosened his grip. "May I escort you back to the ground?"

Arielle nodded. She'd be happy to let him escort her almost anywhere. After assisting her back down the stairs, the duke seemed in no rush to get back to the others. Arielle didn't mind; a few moments alone with Marsham were exactly what she wanted. They strolled a roundabout route at a leisurely pace.

"Your Grace," Arielle began hesitantly. There hadn't been a good time before now to ask about their shared past, and now she was torn. She was afraid to hear his answer and simultaneously unable to bear not knowing. "Have we—have we met? I mean, before the Old Ship?" He frowned in confusion, and Arielle stammered on, blushing. "I—I remember very little about my life before I came to Lady Priscilla, but you look so—so familiar that I wondered…"

"I'm afraid not." He smiled, the gorgeous smile that so easily melted her, then considered a moment. "There is something about you that catches my mind, but I can't think why. I know we haven't been introduced before you arrived here—believe me, I'd remember you."

Arielle bit back her disappointment. She'd hoped for an easy answer, like something she'd find in a novel—a confession that they'd been in love, perhaps, and that he only hadn't said anything because he was afraid she'd forgotten him along with the rest of her past. But no, nothing so simple.

They wandered on a moment, then he asked, "You really remember nothing of your past?"

Arielle shook her head. "Very little. There are things I can guess: I think I had no family, and I hadn't danced before Olivia taught me. And I've had little experience with horses."

"That must be a frustratingly piecemeal way to discover things."

"That's why I was hoping you remembered me and could tell me more." Arielle met his sympathetic eyes and shrugged, unwilling to ruin their moment together with negativity. "Your being unable to do so leaves me no worse off than I was."

They were approaching the rest of the group, now all clustered in the shade. Arielle was disappointed that Marsham had no knowledge to give her, but she was grateful for the chance to ask. She was also grateful for a few minutes alone with him. If he was her true love, if they were to marry before her time was up, she had to make the most of any time together.

The reactions to their return were varied. Mrs. Goulding's expression was sour again, though her daughter echoed Olivia's cry that they'd been worried about Arielle and had begun to consider sending out a search party. Lord Patrick's face was the same expressionless mask that Arielle had seen when he'd first introduced her to his brother. The other two gentlemen said nothing but hid their irritation poorly. Were they jealous or impatient? Then Mr. Sharpton suggested that it was high time to head to the inn, and she decided it must be the latter. Perhaps wandering about the beautiful grounds of a castle was meager entertainment to a sporting gentleman.

The inn wasn't far, and before long they were settled in a private parlor with cold meats and salads, fruits and tarts, ale and lemonade. Arielle ate and listened to the conversation around her, but she didn't participate in it unless someone—usually Letitia—asked her a direct question. The room was crowded and loud and hot, and the smells of food and sweat and ale blended unpleasantly. Arielle's head began to ache, and she wished she could go back to the top of the castle wall and breathe the free, fresh air again all by herself. Finally, unable to take another minute, she turned to Aunt Prissy, who was seated to her right.

"Will you walk outside with me?" she whispered.

With a knowing smile, Aunt Prissy rose, and together they left the bustling inn to walk about the yard.

"Thank you." Arielle heaved a deep breath and let it out in a sigh. "I just…"

"I understand, dear. You're still new here, and I'd guess that you were on your own for goodness knows how long before you came. This life takes some getting used to."

A step sounded behind them. Aunt Prissy paused and turned. Lord Patrick had followed them out. He came close enough to speak softly.

"Are you well, Miss Arielle?"

Color rose in her cheeks, that anyone else should have noticed her weakness. "A headache, my lord," she said. "From the sun earlier…"

"And the noise and heat inside," he guessed. "Shall I take you home?"

Arielle shook her head as adamantly as her headache would allow. "No, please, I don't want to break up the party. I'll be fine if I just walk for a bit, I'm sure."

He nodded, though he looked unconvinced. "May I join you, then? It is too stuffy for me in there."

They accepted, and he offered an arm to Lady Priscilla. The three of them strolled together across the yard and back. The fresh air helped, but despite her bonnet, the sun hurt Arielle's eyes. She tilted her head down, but it couldn't completely shut out all the chaos of a busy posting inn.

"Lord Patrick," Aunt Prissy said when they'd reached the front door again, "would you be so good as to tell my niece I'm not feeling quite the thing and would like to go home?"

"It would be my privilege."

He was gone inside before Arielle could say a word in argument. And what would she have said? She could hardly decide for her guardian how that lady felt or what to do about it. She'd sound utterly heartless. Arielle sighed and decided to be grateful to both of them for giving her this escape without making her feel worse about it.

When Lord Patrick returned with Olivia, his landau was brought around. As he handed them in, Olivia said, "Would you mind taking a short detour, Lord Patrick, to show Ari the priory?"

Olivia had feigned obliviousness to Arielle's condition, which the girl appreciated as she didn't want anyone to fuss over her, but Olivia's voice was pitched lower than usual when she spoke.

Lord Patrick gave Arielle an inquiring look, and she nodded. So he said, "It would be no trouble at all, Miss Farley."

They turned the opposite way out of the inn yard and in a few minutes were stopping in the shade of a stand of trees. A wide, well-trimmed meadow stretched between them and the jagged remains of ancient stone walls.

"This was once a Benedictine monastery," Lord Patrick said, turning in his seat and speaking quietly. "Also built by William de Warrenne."

"Aren't the ruins magical?" Olivia leaned over to Arielle. "I can't see them without thinking of Camelot, and about Gawain and Galahad, and Tristan and Lady Isolde."

## CHAPTER 9

Arielle turned her blank look from Lord Patrick to Olivia. "Who?"

"Oh, but you haven't read about King Arthur yet, have you?" Olivia cast her gaze over the ruins, as if asking them why Arielle couldn't see what she saw. She shook her head. "That's it, then. I insist on choosing the next book to read aloud."

"Will it be Malory," Aunt Prissy asked with a wry smile, "or Chretien de Troyes?"

"Probably de Troyes," Olivia responded, unbothered. "I don't know if you'll survive another time through Malory."

Lord Patrick was listening to this whole exchange from his seat on the box with laughter in his eyes. He turned to Arielle then and asked quietly, "What do you think of the ruins?"

Arielle was studying the scene before her. "It *is* magical, even if I don't know what Camelot is. And it's sad. I wonder how many lives were held within it while it stood, and how many more it has watched pass as it crumbled."

A smile curved Lord Patrick's mouth. "Those are deeper reflections than my own," he admitted. "I was thinking it would be a good place for a picnic."

Arielle smiled. "It is that too."

They set off again, and Arielle rested her head back against the seat and closed her eyes.

# Chapter 10

The next evening, Arielle went with the Farleys to the Steine for the weekly tea and promenade. Her headache had gone away after an evening of resting quietly. The first people they met as they walked were Letitia Goulding and Miss Crewe. Aunt Prissy nodded her permission, and Arielle joined her friend. She didn't know Miss Crewe well, but she seemed like a sweet girl, if extraordinarily empty-headed.

"What happened yesterday?" Letitia demanded immediately. "You left so suddenly and so early!"

Arielle bit her lip. "Aunt Prissy declared that she wasn't feeling quite the thing," she said truthfully. "She asked Lord Patrick to take us home."

"How dreadful to have an infirm old lady as your guardian," Miss Crewe said sympathetically. "She must put such a damper on your fun."

"Not at all," Arielle said coolly. "Aunt Prissy is a dear, and she's hardly infirm. Only it had been a long day, and the sun was hot."

"Of course," Letitia said soothingly. "No one could ever think poorly of Lady Priscilla. But, Arielle, your leaving early meant that you didn't get to hear what Mama is planning. I was just discussing it with Miss Crewe."

"What is it?"

"A special dinner party," Letitia said. "She's been planning to host a dinner for weeks, but she just decided to change the plans from cards after dinner to a kind of musicale. Well, not quite—it doesn't all have to be music. She's asking all the young ladies to display their accomplishments after dinner. I'll be doing my best illusion spell."

"And I'll be singing," Miss Crewe put in. "Miss Rowles, you know, plays the pianoforte, and we've been practicing a French song together."

Arielle's heart sank as the girls talked, and it must have shown on her face.

"Whatever is the matter? Isn't it a wonderful scheme?" Letitia said. She leaned closer and murmured, "Mama already got His Grace to agree to come."

Arielle saw the whole situation with sudden clarity. Mrs. Goulding was jealous of any attention Arielle received from Marsham—she wanted Letitia to secure the most eligible bachelor in Brighton as well as the title of duchess. Arielle wouldn't have believed it of her, but the sour expression her friend's mother had worn several times supported her suspicion that the woman had planned her party's entertainment in order to show her daughter to advantage while embarrassing Arielle before the duke. Mrs. Goulding knew perfectly well that Arielle had no accomplishments to showcase.

Feeling both girls' eyes on her, Arielle stammered, "I—I think we'll be unable to come."

A cry went up at this. "Why ever not?"

Arielle wished she didn't have to admit it before Miss Crewe, but she supposed it didn't matter: half of Brighton already knew the truth. "I have no accomplishments," she muttered.

"None?" Miss Crewe looked bemused. "You can't play the pianoforte?"

"Not a note."

"The harp?"

Arielle had never even seen a harp and wasn't quite sure what they were. She shook her head.

"Can you sing?"

Another head shake.

"What about magic?" Letitia said. "I have some easy spells you could master quickly."

"I've never tried," Arielle said.

Letitia frowned. "But this is awful. And Mama insisted I invite you most particularly."

Arielle bit her lip and looked away, but Letitia didn't miss the reaction.

"No, you can't mean… Mama would never do it apurpose! Why would she?"

"Does she want you to marry a duke?"

Miss Crewe laughed. "Well, naturally. Every mama wants their daughters to marry well."

But Letitia looked thoughtful. "You think Mama arranged it so that, not only would I amaze the company, but you would look worse by comparison?"

Arielle shrugged.

"Hmph." Letitia scowled. "I refuse to let you be humiliated, whatever anyone's plans are. You're my dearest friend. We will *find* you an accomplishment."

"That's not necessary," Arielle said. "I can decline the invitation just as easily."

"And do what? If you don't go to the party, what is there to do?" Miss Crewe looked genuinely curious. Arielle wondered if the girl had a single original thought in her head or the slightest ability to entertain herself.

"I often read to Aunt Prissy and Livvie in the evenings while they sew, and they're soon going to teach me to sew too."

"That's it!"

Arielle looked at her friend in surprise. "Sewing?"

Letitia grinned. "No—reading! You love books—I know you would read them all day if you weren't dragged out to be social with the rest of us."

Arielle blushed, but she couldn't deny the truth of this. Her favorite part of each day was when she had time to curl up in the sitting room with a new book, especially when Hessy found her and jumped, purring, onto her lap. On an ideal day, she'd stop reading only to go to the kitchen and coax Mrs. Little into letting her help make a new treat. She'd discovered a fascination with cooking and how foods changed from start to finish, particularly when the oven was involved. The cook had allowed her to help make pound cake, sweet rolls, and cherry tarts, and when they'd finished baking, she'd sent either Mary or Lindsay with a tray of the treats to the sitting room—for her to snack on while reading.

"Pick a passage to read aloud. Only a few pages: something amusing or beautiful or romantic." Letitia's eyes were alight with enthusiasm. "What are you reading now?"

"I've just gotten *Pride and Prejudice* from the library, but I haven't begun reading it yet."

"Well, the dinner is on Saturday, so you have a whole week to find a passage to read."

Arielle was beginning to wish that she was home reading Miss Austen's book right now rather than being coerced into performing by her friend. She shrugged noncommittally.

Miss Crewe was called away then by Miss Rowles and Mrs. Ingersoll. Arielle and Letitia were almost immediately joined by the Duke of Marsham.

"How glad I am to find you both here!" The smile on that handsome face had all the brilliance of the noonday sun, and Arielle thought she might melt. "It was too bad you had to leave early yesterday, Miss Arielle, but that's all right, because the fun will continue! I'm having a private card party on Wednesday—a little dinner beforehand, then a proper evening of games. You will both come, won't you?"

Letitia agreed readily. Arielle professed herself eager to attend but that she must apply to her guardian before accepting.

"Quite right, of course. Invitations will be sent round tomorrow. I do hope to see you both there."

They all bowed, and he walked on. The girls soon met up with some others of Miss Goulding's acquaintance, and Arielle defected to return to her guardians. After the headache of the day before, Aunt Prissy had decided that they would take their tea at home. They turned and made their way back along the Steine and Marine Parade, talking all the while.

The promised invitations came the next morning. Olivia accepted the duke's on behalf of her and Arielle; Aunt Prissy had already promised to visit with Lady Caroline that evening. When Olivia read out Mrs. Goulding's invitation, Arielle hesitantly voiced her suspicions of the reason behind the entertainment. Neither woman disagreed with her, but Aunt Prissy shook her head and muttered, "Nonsensical woman." The invitation, however, was accepted, once Arielle had explained Letitia's suggestion that she read an excerpt from a novel.

## CHAPTER 10

"Oh, do, Ari! That's perfect," Olivia agreed. "You read aloud so well."

Olivia's praise, and the fact that neither member of her new family thought her suspicions were faulty, encouraged Arielle. She read with renewed purpose, though it was impossible to read more often than she already did.

That evening, as they settled into the parlor after dinner, Olivia bent over the basket of mending, choosing what to sew. She pulled out Arielle's walking dress.

"What's this, Ari? What happened?"

"I stepped on the hem at the castle," Arielle said. Her cheeks warmed as she remembered the duke's strong form behind her, keeping her from tumbling off the wall. "Lindsay noticed later that I'd torn it."

Olivia and Aunt Prissy exchanged glances. "When did you step on it, Ari?" Aunt Prissy asked, the wrinkles around her eyes creasing as she smirked. "I'm sensing a story here."

"Not much of one." Arielle told them what had happened on the castle wall.

"What were you doing on the wall in the first place?" Olivia stared, horrified. "You could have fallen to your death, and then what would we do?"

"I didn't fall," Arielle protested. "His Grace kept me from falling, and I probably wouldn't have even wobbled if he hadn't startled me."

They all stared at each other for a silent moment, then Olivia giggled. "It is rather romantic, a rescue on a castle wall."

Arielle blushed. She'd thought the same. Her feelings for Marsham were warm but confused, and she didn't think she ought to tell the Farleys about what she remembered regarding him. She decided to change the subject. "Speaking of romance, did you have stories about Camel-something for us tonight?"

"Camelot, yes!" Olivia dropped the dress back into the mending basket and went to the bookshelf above the mantle.

"Livvie, I think you should read tonight," Aunt Prissy said. "They're your stories, after all, and I think it's time I teach Ari how to sew so she can mend her own hems."

Arielle moved to sit beside Lady Priscilla, who showed her how to thread a needle and tie a knot in the end of the thread. Then she took a bit of cotton fabric from the scrap bag and showed Arielle how to move the needle in and out. Olivia began reading then, the story of Eric and Enide. It was pleasant sitting like this, just the three of them in the firelight, with a window open to let in the breeze off the Channel. Arielle pricked her finger with the needle more times than she wanted to admit, but it was nice to have her hands busy, and she was glad to learn a useful skill. Her stitches were uneven, but they improved over the course of the evening. Aunt Prissy even taught her two other types of stitches and explained that each was useful in different circumstances. When Arielle had filled her scrap of cotton with lines of seams that were more or less straight, Olivia passed her the torn dress. Aunt Prissy showed her how to pin the torn place and sew the hem. It wasn't the most beautiful seam, and Arielle knew that anyone looking closely would be able to see the difference—her repaired section puckered just a bit—but she felt a hint of pride at having done it herself.

# Chapter 11

On Tuesday morning, Lady Priscilla went sea-bathing. She went twice a week, in the mornings on Tuesdays and Fridays, in the machines at the western end of town. Arielle had climbed inside one of the machines—one of the big, wooden, horse-drawn boxes—during her first week with the Farleys but had immediately climbed back out before it could move. It was too dark and enclosed, and the thought of water seeping in as it rolled into the waves horrified her. Instead, she had taken to walking on the beach while her guardian was dipped in the cool water. Sometimes Olivia accompanied her, but sometimes Olivia stayed home to write letters or receive callers. Lindsay came with Arielle then. The first thing Aunt Prissy and Olivia had drilled into her was that a lady never walked out alone. Much as she valued freedom, Arielle willingly abided by this rule: she was still so new to Brighton and everything in it, and she found even the abigail's presence comforting. Some days she simply sat on the beach and watched the waves roll in, soaking in their soothing rhythm as her skirts were kissed by the incoming tide. In moments like these it was easy to forget her fear of being unaccomplished, Mrs. Goulding's spite, even the Duke of Marsham himself. The water called to Arielle, sang to her soul, and left her longing for something on the very edge of memory.

***

On Wednesday evening, Arielle and Olivia walked to Marsham's house on the Steine and were welcomed in. They were twenty to table, including everyone who had been on the Lewes Castle expedition. Arielle was seated between Lord Preston and a Mr. Haskins, whom she hadn't met previously. Mr. Haskins was not chatty; his full attention was on his copious servings of food and drink. Lord Preston was attentive but dull. He was an earl in his middle thirties and generally thought to be a good sort of person. He had ambitions to be a Corinthian like His Grace of Marsham, and it seemed to Arielle that he rather idolized the man. Arielle couldn't entirely blame him: Marsham was easy to idealize into the perfect specimen of manhood. He sat at the head of the table in his flawlessly tailored suit with his dark hair carelessly mussed, a wide smile on his face, and his dark eyes alight.

In each of their previous meetings, Arielle had found him almost entrancing. But tonight, for the first time, she found something mildly off-putting. She couldn't quite put her finger on it, but whatever it was only got stronger as dinner progressed and the wine flowed freely. He was obviously in his element. But he was perhaps a little too boisterous, a little too loud, a little too willing to boast about his winning racehorses or his bouts in the ring against Gentleman Jackson. She preferred him the way he'd been at the castle, when he'd pulled her back from the edge and walked with her alone, or the way he'd spoken to her and Letitia on the Steine: enthusiastic but not over the top.

After dinner, the ladies repaired to the drawing room for half an hour before the gentlemen joined them again. The Duke of Marsham rallied all whist players and gathered them in a separate parlor. Olivia joined them, being fond of the game, and left Arielle with Letitia. The rest of the party settled on a lively game of lottery tickets. Arielle shot her friend a nervous look.

"You've never played it before, have you?" Letitia leaned over and whispered. Arielle shook her head. "Not to worry—I'll help you."

The two sat next to each other, and while Mrs. Ingersoll distributed the fish, Letitia quietly explained the rules of the game. Lord Patrick, with a warm smile, positioned himself nearby. The game commenced, and Letitia continued to give Arielle pointers as they played. The group was spirited, exuberant, and though Arielle laughed with the rest, she found herself overwhelmed long before anyone else appeared to tire of the noise. She felt another headache coming on. The clock on the mantle said it was past ten o'clock, which was the Farleys' usual hour for bed.

When the game ended and everyone prepared for another round, Arielle begged off and stood. "I need to speak with Livvie for a moment," she told Letitia. "I'll skip this round."

As she squeezed out of her seat and past the others, Lord Patrick said, "Can I help you with anything, Miss Arielle?"

"Will you point me in the direction of the whist parlor?"

Rather than telling her the way, he left with her, guiding her to the parlor's open door. Before she could walk through it, though, he put a hand on her arm.

"Before you go..." His voice was very low and almost shy.

"Will you save me a waltz tomorrow?"

Arielle hadn't expected that, but she smiled and agreed readily. Lord Patrick removed his hand, bowed slightly, and disappeared back into the drawing room.

Arielle stepped into the parlor and over to Olivia's seat. "Livvie, can I speak to you a moment?"

Olivia looked up at her, studied her briefly, and said, "We're nearly done this hand, and then it will be time for us to go home. Can you wait just that long?"

"Of course."

Arielle moved away to stand by the door. When Olivia joined her, Marsham came too. He wouldn't allow them to walk home, insisting that his driver take them in his carriage. "It's too dark for such lovely ladies to be walking." His eyes held Arielle's, and she blushed. "I hope, Miss Arielle, that you'll do me the honor of the first dance tomorrow night."

She stammered an acceptance. When they were in the carriage for the short ride home, Olivia asked, "Now, was there something you wanted to talk about, or did you just need to get away?"

"Am I that predictable?"

Olivia shrugged. "You looked like you needed to get away."

Arielle sighed. "I did. Letitia was wonderful, and I enjoyed the game, but it was just too much after a while. I wish people would have smaller, quieter parties—I'd like those."

Olivia smiled. "Perhaps we'll have to host one ourselves, then."

\*\*\*

Patrick stayed at his brother's house until the last of the guests were gone. He wanted to talk to Michael, and he knew that the duke would not be in any condition tomorrow morning. When they had the drawing room to themselves, Michael lounged on a chair with his leg flung over the arm.

"Bee in your bonnet, brother? Let's have it out."

Patrick paced the length of the room. "Who were you telling your stories for at dinner? Who were you aiming to impress?"

"The whole room." Michael waved expansively. At Patrick's glare, he shook his head. "Does it matter?"

"You were watching Miss Goulding's and Miss Arielle's reactions most closely."

"Very well, then. I wasn't trying to impress the *whole* room, just the prettiest ladies in it."

Patrick stifled an exasperated sigh. He hated talking to his brother when he was foxed. "Are you just flirting like usual, or do you actually intend to marry this time?" His stomach knotted, and he wished he could avoid the subject, but he had to know.

"You sound like Mother."

"Answer the question."

"A duchy needs an heir," Michael shrugged. "It seems I've finally decided to find myself a duchess."

The knots in his gut tightened. "Which of them will it be?"

"Sorry?"

"Miss Goulding or Miss Arielle. Which one? You can't keep stringing them both along like this."

Michael was silent for a long time. Then he scrubbed a hand over his face and sighed. "Miss Goulding is perfect in every way, an unmistakable diamond of the first water. But Arielle Farley is… enchanting. She's quiet and self-contained and vulnerable—my opposite in so many ways—and there's something more about her… If I were anyone else…"

Patrick had involuntarily held his breath as his brother

described Arielle, silently praying that Michael had no intentions toward her. The two would be a miserable pair. Once Michael made his vows, he would be faithful—probably—but the crowds that Michael thrived in would be too much for Arielle. His brother's social lifestyle would crush her within months.

Patrick couldn't bear the thought. Arielle was everything his brother said, and she was also bright and intelligent. She was curious and open and engaging. She had a laugh that he couldn't forget and wanted to hear more of.

He heard the word Michael had left unspoken, and he needed to hear it said aloud. "But…"

Michael took a deep breath. "But… I'm *not* anyone else. And a duke must marry a diamond."

He got to his feet and moved to the doorway. He paused with his hand on the frame and looked back at Patrick. "I will stop giving Miss Arielle extra attention. I've already asked her for the first dance tomorrow, but it won't go beyond that."

With that, he left, and Patrick showed himself out.

\*\*\*

Elizabeth Alexander, the Dowager Duchess of Marsham, arrived in Marine Parade at noon the next day.

"You made good time, Mother," Patrick said, kissing her cheek.

"I've made this trip so many times I could do it in my sleep," she said dismissively. "And I had to make sure I didn't miss the ball at the Old Ship tonight. Caroline tells me that the Castle isn't holding them this year. Pity." Patrick made an inarticulate, soothing sound. "I'll get settled and rest a while, then we'll see your brother at the ball, won't we?"

Patrick nodded. "Remind me again why you're staying with me and not Michael, Mother? I thought you meant to superintend him finally finding a wife and settling down." He didn't mention his brother's intention to do just that, or anything about Miss Goulding. Michael could tell her, if Lady Caroline Hervey hadn't already written their mother with the news as gossip.

"I like Marine Parade better than the Steine, of course, and the hours Michael keeps are too late for an old lady like me." She wasn't a day above fifty, and she looked even younger, so Patrick only raised an eyebrow. "Don't you want me here, Patrick?"

He relented. "Of course I do, Mother." He only hoped that her staying with him wouldn't incline her to meddle in his own romantic life.

They arrived early at the Old Ship that evening, as Her Grace was punctual to a fault. She spent the first half hour greeting old acquaintances. Michael arrived only moments before the first dance began. He claimed Arielle's hand and led her to the floor before even noticing his family's presence. Patrick felt the familiar lurch that came with watching them dance together, watching Arielle gaze up worshipfully with those big, beautiful eyes. He turned away and found his mother frowning at the dancers.

"Who is your brother dancing with?" she asked Patrick. "I've never seen her before."

"Lady Priscilla's ward. This is only her third or fourth week in Brighton."

"I didn't know Lady Priscilla had a ward." The duchess's brows climbed. "I'll have to speak with her. Do you know—is she the only one in love, or does he like her too?"

Patrick's stomach sank at her words, but he managed, "He claims to have no serious designs on her."

"Hmm." She turned away, and Patrick was left alone with his bitter thoughts.

His eyes were drawn back to the couple on the floor as though by magnets. The words "is she the only one in love" echoed in his head, over and over. Arielle's feelings for Michael were obvious. And even though the duke had promised not to show her special attention, he couldn't hide his own admiration. Patrick felt sick. The idea of Arielle marrying his brother made him want to emigrate to America and not come back. To see her only as a sister, to watch her discover that Michael was entirely wrong for her and sink into misery while he, Patrick, was the one she ought to be with... It couldn't be borne.

But Michael wouldn't marry her. He had a duty to the duchy and the bloodline. Patrick wouldn't need to move to America. But it would break the poor girl's heart not to be chosen by the man she loved.

Patrick forced himself to turn away, to find another young lady to beg for the next dance, a reel. He pushed his unhappy reflections to the back of his mind. There was nothing he could do to prevent at least one heart from breaking, and it was better not to borrow trouble from tomorrow.

It was both harder and easier to keep those reflections away when it was time to waltz with Arielle. Her sweet, open innocence made him dread the heartbreak he knew would come. But his senses filled with her as they flew around the room, their feet barely seeming to touch the floor. She fit perfectly in his arms and responded to his leading as if they were one creature. In this moment, the future didn't matter. Patrick executed a tricky turn. He felt Arielle's breath catch, then she released it in a laugh. Not the uncontrolled hilarity he'd overheard, but a light, genuine, joyful sound that made his heart beat erratically.

How could Michael—how could *anyone*—walk away from her?

The dance ended. They separated to dance again with other partners. Patrick was escorting Miss Crewe from the floor after a quadrille when they passed his mother and Mrs. Goulding. A bit of Mrs. Goulding's conversation caught his ear.

"...out of nowhere, seemingly. She's a sweet, pretty sort of girl, I'll admit, but who is she, really? I think she must be the natural daughter of one of Lady Priscilla's nephews..."

Patrick stiffened and half turned, but his mother caught his eye. The slightest lifting of her eyebrows stalled him. He took a slow breath and delivered Miss Crewe to her chaperone. When he returned to his mother's side, Mrs. Goulding was walking away. He glared at her retreating back, offended by the rumors she was spreading about Arielle. Jealousy wasn't a good color on anyone, but Mrs. Goulding wore it particularly badly.

"Everyone has opinions on the young Arielle Farley," his mother said, drawing Patrick's attention. "The one thing I've heard most often is that there seems to be a competition between my sons for her affection."

Warmth rose in Patrick's neck, but he didn't answer. It didn't matter what he said: his mother could see for herself. Whatever Patrick might feel, Arielle loved Michael.

"She's managed to cause rather a fuss, hasn't she?" Her tone was cool and indifferent, but her eyes were bright with interest.

"I'm sure it wasn't intentional."

"No, she seems to be a most unaffected girl. I should like to meet her. Pity she oughtn't to be a duchess."

Patrick said nothing.

# Chapter 12

On Saturday evening, Arielle entered the Goulding house with all the confidence she could muster and with the first volume of *Pride and Prejudice* tucked into her reticule. She'd decided to read the section when Jane is ill at Netherfield Park and Elizabeth goes to stay with her. There was some good dialogue between Lizzy and Darcy, and reading through it had made her smile. But when she saw the rest of the company assembling, and she counted the number of places set at the dining table, she wished she could take the book and find a quiet corner to read by herself.

Letitia was at her side within minutes of her arrival. "Are you ready? Did you bring it?"

Arielle nodded. "I shouldn't have let you talk me into this. I should have stayed home. How can I read in front of all these people?"

"Just read to me," her friend said. "I'm not frightening, and I'll sit right in front." Arielle softened, and Letitia tried one more argument to win her over. "I don't see how Mama could have taken a dislike to you—it's absurd—but you can't let her win, not when Marsham and his mother are both here to see."

It was the wrong thing to say. Arielle had known the duke would be present, but—"His mother?" she squeaked.

"Yes, the dowager duchess." Letitia pointed surreptitiously to a thin woman of medium height who had the same light brown hair as Patrick and the same dark eyes as the duke. Her features were more delicate than theirs, but the resemblance was there. Lord Patrick stood beside her, his hands clasped behind his back. Marsham himself was on the other side of the room, chatting animatedly with a cluster of other guests.

"I just met her today," Letitia said. "She's no more alarming than I am."

Arielle disagreed. She'd lain awake for over an hour each night since the card party on Wednesday, trying to figure out how she felt about His Grace. He was everything she'd dreamed of, but there was a niggle of doubt over whether he was actually her true love. She wanted him to be, but she needed to be certain because whatever magic had brought her here and erased her memories depended on it. If there *was* something between them, and if it had any hope of leading to marriage, his mother's approval would be essential.

Arielle could hardly eat at dinner, and her nearest neighbors probably thought her rude, because she only heard one word in four that anyone said, and her responses were monosyllables. The ladies retired to the drawing room first, soon to be joined by the gentlemen, and everyone settled in for the evening's entertainment. The order of young ladies was prearranged by Mrs. Goulding, and Arielle was impressed by the cleverness and elegance of the woman's spite. They sat through a few songs, one of which was the French number performed by Miss Crewe and Miss Rowles. The only two young ladies left were Arielle and Letitia, and when Mrs. Goulding invited Arielle to the front with a poorly concealed smirk, Arielle knew that her friend's mother expected her to back down. She was

## CHAPTER 12

supposed to excuse herself from performing, preferably in the most mortifying manner possible, and Letitia would swoop in to showcase her magic and astound the company.

Instead, Arielle thanked Mrs. Goulding politely, pulled the book from her reticule, and got to her feet. Her hands were ice cold, and her knees shook, but she made it to stand near the pianoforte. Mrs. Goulding's smug look had faded. Letitia smiled and nodded encouragingly from her seat in the front. Arielle wished the room were not so brightly lit: she could see everyone. The Duke of Marsham lounged back in his chair; his mother sat forward, curious and attentive. Lord Patrick watched Arielle intently, and she darted her gaze away from them. But it didn't matter who she looked at—they were all looking at *her*. She couldn't breathe. Her fingers were too numb and stiff to open the book.

But then her eyes found Olivia and Lady Priscilla. Aunt Prissy winked and pretended to sew, and Olivia grinned. *Just like at home*, they were saying. *You read to us every evening; do it again now.*

Arielle took a shaky breath. They were right. This didn't have to be any different from a quiet evening at home. She would keep her eyes on the page and read to her guardians—her family.

Opening the book to the page she'd marked with a blue ribbon may have been the hardest thing Arielle had ever done. Another deep breath, and she began to read. The second sentence was easier; the third, easier still. By the end of the paragraph, Arielle had almost forgotten all the watching eyes. A tiny smile pulled at her mouth as she relived her favorite part of this first volume: Darcy was falling in love with Lizzy, and Lizzy had no idea.

She finished reading the excerpt she'd planned and bit her lip as she closed the book. She raised her eyes hesitantly, looking first for Olivia and Aunt Prissy, who beamed at her, and then Letitia, who eagerly began the applause. Arielle stumbled back to her seat, her legs like jelly.

"You were brilliant," Letitia whispered as her mother called her up.

Arielle hugged the book to her chest and sat back to watch her friend.

Letitia showed no signs of struggling with the same fears as Arielle. She met the eyes of the gathered audience, smiling at them, before speaking a single word. The candles all snuffed out at once. Gasps and a few low cries filled the air until the candles relit at another word. But they looked different to Arielle somehow. She frowned at the candle nearest her, so she was already watching closely when Letitia's next word lifted the flames off of the wicks and drew all the lights to herself. They swirled over her head like an enormous turban, making her curls glow like molten gold. The lights spread farther out, enclosing Letitia in a sphere of dancing, winking lights. Another word; the lights began to fade from red-gold to a sickly yellow-green, and then to the rich green of summer grass. From there they continued to aqua, then azure, and then violet. Back through primrose and peach before returning to the proper rosy gold of flames. With another word, Letitia sent all the tiny flames back to their candles, where they promptly went out again. A final word, and the candles flickered back into life, looking real and normal this time.

The applause for Letitia's illusion was more enthusiastic than for any of the others, and rightly so, Arielle thought. The magic had been breathtaking. She stood and hugged her friend when

## CHAPTER 12

Mrs. Goulding declared the performances at an end.

"That was amazing. I may let you teach me magic after all."

Letitia laughed and was drawn away to speak with the Duke of Marsham and the dowager duchess. Arielle began to make her way between the chairs and sofas to join Aunt Prissy, but her shakiness from earlier hadn't quite worn off, and she dropped her book. It landed on the floor in front of a brocade upholstered sofa. When she fumbled to pick it up, it slid farther under, so that Arielle had to drop to her knees and crawl halfway under the sofa to get it. She was just extricating herself from the awkward position when she heard voices overhead on the other side of the couch.

"You planned a spiteful trick, Celine. It's plain to anyone with eyes that you were trying to humiliate my Arielle." Aunt Prissy's voice was sharper than Arielle had ever heard it.

"I don't know why you're complaining, Lady Priscilla. The girl came through admirably."

"Of course she did," Aunt Prissy snapped. "I never doubted her. I simply didn't expect such conduct from *you*."

Arielle crouched uncomfortably under the couch, afraid to move in case one of them should notice her.

"Oh, please, don't pretend you wouldn't have done the same in my place." Mrs. Goulding's voice dripped with disdain. "Letitia deserves to be a duchess, and she will be. To tell the truth, I don't know why I bothered. 'Your Arielle' doesn't stand a chance. Mysterious bloodline, no dowry, no name of any value… She'll be lucky to make an average match, let alone snare a duke."

Arielle bit her lip as she heard the rustle of cloth as Mrs. Goulding swept away from Aunt Prissy. She wanted to shoot to her feet and give the woman a piece of her mind—she was a *Farley*, and that was a name of *great* value—but before she could, she had to back out from under the couch. And by the time she managed that, the truth of Mrs. Goulding's words hit home.

The Duke of Marsham was one of the most illustrious personages in England. He needed to marry a young lady with connections, with fortune, with a bloodline so clean you could lick it. And Arielle had none of those things. Even her connection to the Farleys was fabricated, a borrowed family, a borrowed name.

No matter how she felt about him, no matter how he felt about her, he couldn't marry her.

Aunt Prissy had turned away from the sofa, so she didn't see Arielle get to her feet. Arielle had a second to compose herself before she laid a hand on Aunt Prissy's arm and asked in a whisper if they could go home. Before hearing Mrs. Goulding's words, Arielle had thought to join Letitia with Marsham and his mother—maybe seeing him in this company would ease her mind about whatever had unsettled her at the card party. Now, however, her mind spun, and she needed time alone to think, to process what she'd heard. Lord Patrick moved toward them as if eager to speak with her, but she couldn't look at him as she slipped from the room. He could read her emotions far too well, and she couldn't bear his concern or sympathy.

Arielle cried herself to sleep that night. She cried out her relief that her performance was over, her anger over Mrs. Goulding's hurtful words, her loss of hope in Marsham. She had never felt so helpless, so worthless in the eyes of society.

She slept late the next morning, and no one disturbed her. Even Hessy seemed aware of her need for comfort. He snuggled closer and purred gently, letting her stroke his silky

## CHAPTER 12

fur. Her eyes were puffy and stiff when she finally rose, but she splashed water over her face and pushed open the shutters on her window. She leaned out and inhaled deeply of the salty air. After a few deep breaths, she felt lighter. It was impossible to hold onto the emotions of the night before with the sun on her face and the sea breeze ruffling her hair.

No connections? No family? She had Aunt Prissy and Livvie, and they loved her. They'd *chosen* to be her family.

A scheming mama trying to bring her down? Well, she hadn't succeeded in humiliating Arielle last night, and if Mrs. Goulding managed to arrange her daughter an advantageous marriage, so much the better. Letitia would make an impeccable duchess.

This last gave Arielle pause. Her chest ached when she thought of Marsham. He was so beautiful and strong and charming. She'd probably always melt when he smiled at her. But at times she'd wondered if he wasn't quite what she wanted. He was too boisterous, too outgoing. He drank more than she liked, and he showed little interest in books.

But he danced like a god. She sighed and rested her elbow on the windowsill and her chin in her hand. A marriage couldn't be built on dancing, not when her mysterious magic required true love. Maybe Letitia was his best choice after all, much as she hated to let Mrs. Goulding have her way.

By the time Arielle came downstairs, Aunt Prissy and Olivia were at church. Lindsay said they'd wanted to let Arielle rest after the many late nights. Arielle was grateful. She needed a day without people. She took Lindsay with her to the beach, leaving the abigail to sit within sight while she walked in the surf and let the waves wash away any lingering bitterness. Arielle wouldn't burden her friends with worry for her. Nobody needed to know what she'd overheard or that she'd just learned that the man she thought she might love was off limits. Especially not Letitia. Letitia was her closest friend, and she wouldn't let jealousy, or even a suspicion of jealousy, tear them apart. She admired and respected the other girl and wanted her to be happy, even if it meant that Letitia got to marry Marsham.

"I can't really be in love, then, can I?" she said to a gull perched on a pile of seaweed left by the high tide. It hopped closer, its beady eye regarding her calculatingly. "If I were, I'd be a jealous, heartbroken mess. I'm like Lizzy realizing that she never loved Wickham, though Marsham is so much better than Wickham ever could be." The bird cocked its head. Arielle laughed. "It's from *Pride and Prejudice*, though I don't know why I'm explaining to a bird. And, no, I don't have any food for you."

Arielle stayed on the beach for hours. Her thoughts always came clearer to the rhythm of the surf, and she had a lot of tangled thoughts to work through.

"If I know after only two weeks that I don't love His Grace, I must not have known him long in my life before—long enough for him to look familiar, but short enough that I still thought I loved him." She murmured to the sea, letting the waves carry her secrets away as they rolled back out.

If she didn't love Marsham, then she still had to find her true love before she could marry him within the year, which felt like a monumental task. And how was Marsham connected to her past? He'd said they'd never met before, and yet, his was one of the two faces she'd remembered.

She sighed and sat on the stones and hugged her knees to her chest, tucking her skirts around her.

The connection between Marsham and her past was frail

as spider silk. It was foolish to hope that she still might learn something from him, even though he wouldn't help her fulfill the magic's requirements. But the unknown tugged at her—her missing memories and the uncertain future consequences if she failed to find her true love—and Marsham was the only link she had.

# Chapter 13

The next morning, Arielle walked to the Marine Library alone. Aunt Prissy and Olivia were both busy, Lindsay was with them, and Arielle couldn't wait another minute to get her hands on Miss Austen's next volume. She borrowed a book of poems by Cowper as well, since Aunt Prissy had gamely put up with *Udolpho* and Arthurian Romances for the last two weeks. Arielle had no experience with poetry, but the librarian was sure Lady Priscilla would enjoy it. She paused at the door to look back and wave her thanks, then turned and collided with the gentleman just outside. She dropped her books. He bent to pick them up with her, and her cheeks colored.

"I don't know why I'm always dropping books around you, Lord Patrick," she said, hugging the two volumes to her chest and straightening up.

His eyes sparkled. "It was my fault, I'm sure. If I hadn't been in the way, your books would have been quite safe." He smiled. "What do you have today?"

"The final volume of *Pride and Prejudice* for me and Cowper for Aunt Prissy. Livvie and I have gotten to choose what to read in the evenings already, so now it's her turn."

"Do you read together often?"

"I read to them every night when we're at home."

"That explains it—your performance at the Gouldings' was so exquisite because you've had so much practice."

"Not much practice," she said, embarrassed. "I mean, some, but I would hardly call it exquisite…" Her cheeks grew hot.

Lord Patrick laughed. "Very well. To please you, I will change my compliment, and you can forget the last. I enjoyed your reading very much, and I particularly liked the selection you chose."

"Isn't it a delightful scene?" Talking about books instantly put Arielle on comfortable ground. "I love their conversations."

"So do I. May I give you another compliment?"

Arielle raised one shoulder. She'd rather he didn't—her face might catch fire at any moment—but she was curious all the same.

"My mother said if reading to herself were as enjoyable as listening to you read aloud, she'd visit the lending library every day."

Arielle shook her head and couldn't stop a laugh from escaping. "I see now where you got your gift for flattery."

He gave her a little bow of mock gallantry. She grinned. She wanted to know if Marsham had said anything, but she wouldn't ask. It would appear indelicate, and she probably didn't want to know that he found her reading dull or unworthy of comment.

She moved to step onto the street. Lord Patrick, looking around, stopped her.

"Did you come alone this morning?"

"Please don't tell," she pleaded, eyes wide. "No one else was available, and I couldn't bear to wait. It's only a few blocks."

"I understand the draw of a final volume," he acknowledged.

"But allow me to walk you home. I just need to step inside to get my own book, and we can be on our way."

Arielle thanked him and waited just inside the door while he made his selection. As they stepped out onto the street, she glanced at his book. "What did you get?"

"A biography of Edward the Confessor, the second-to-last Anglo-Saxon king before the Norman Conquest. The last king was his brother-in-law Harold Godwinson, who faced enemies on multiple fronts before William the Conqueror defeated him in October of 1066." Arielle's expression must have gone entirely blank, because Lord Patrick apologized. "I forget that not everyone is as fascinated by history as I am."

"Don't apologize," Arielle said. "I'm rather lost, but that doesn't mean I'm uninterested in what you're saying."

He laughed ruefully. "Everyone looks rather lost when I start discussing history."

Arielle hated that he felt unable to share his interest. He was the sort of person who went out of his way for others, and she wished more people would go out of their way for him. "My excuse is better than most, I think," she said. "I can't remember my own life from a month ago. Names of centuries-old kings are a bit beyond my reach at the moment. Will you tell me about them?"

She watched his face with delight as something within him lit up. He was more animated and charming than she'd ever seen him as he verbally sketched a rough history for her. To her surprise, she found herself following along easily enough. He brought the names and dates to life for her, telling her a story that she could grasp onto. When he mentioned that William the Conqueror landed on English soil at Pevensey, she stopped him.

## CHAPTER 13

"Pevensey? Like your horse?"

He grinned, his cheeks flushing in mild embarrassment. "Exactly."

"And... Hastings, was it?" She tried to remember the name of the second horse, the one she hadn't had time to meet.

"Named for the battle at which William the Conqueror defeated Harold Godwinson."

Arielle laughed, enjoying this glimpse at a side of Lord Patrick she hadn't expected. He chuckled too, and they walked on for a moment in silence. Arielle's mind drifted back to the story that had been occupying her mind so drastically that she'd had to walk out alone this morning, the final volume of which she held in her arms at that moment.

"Is it true, do you think, what Miss Austen says, that a single man in possession of a fortune must want a wife?"

She glanced up at Lord Patrick. His surprise was plain to read, and she thought she saw alarm as well. She went on quickly.

"I only ask out of natural curiosity, because Aunt Prissy informs me that the reverse is *not* true, that a single woman in possession of a fortune has no need of a husband whatsoever."

She grinned at his shocked expression and waited for his reluctant chuckle, which came right on cue.

"I'm sure Lady Priscilla has done very well without one," he said. "For the rest, I daresay I don't know."

They chatted a bit more about books as they walked on. Arielle didn't notice that they'd passed the Farleys' house until they reached the end of Marine Parade and paused to look out over the beach and waves. Arielle felt herself relaxing though she hadn't been especially tense during their walk.

"Do you see those big rocks out there?" Lord Patrick pointed to a cluster of large gray stones that rose out of the water. He clasped his hands and book behind him and frowned. "Earlier in the season, several weeks before you came, Michael was injured on those rocks. I don't know why he was climbing them—probably a wager—but he hit his head hard. He was washed ashore by the rising tide. His friends and I found him unconscious on the beach."

Arielle stared at him, horrified. The ache in her chest that accompanied the mention of His Grace was back. "How awful," she whispered.

Lord Patrick nodded. "He had a sprained ankle as well, and he'd caught a chill that kept him in bed for more than a week. For the first three days, all he'd say in response to our questions was that he'd been rescued by an angel."

Arielle's heartache intensified, but she swallowed it back. She studied her companion's face. He looked thoughtful now, but she remembered how closed off and expressionless he'd become each time he'd seen her and Marsham together, and how she'd wondered if there was some unspoken rift between the brothers.

"Why are you telling me this?" she asked.

"So you don't try to swim at this end of town," he said lightly, shooting her a quick smile. He sobered. "And... because I want you to know. Michael and I have our differences, but I've never been more terrified than when I saw his crumpled body on the beach."

Arielle reached out and laid her hand gently on his arm. "I'm so sorry," she said. "I can't even imagine."

He took her hand in his, then tucked it into the crook of his elbow as if he were escorting her to the dance floor. Arielle wondered if he found the position as reassuring as she did.

## CHAPTER 13

The warm strength of his arm under her hand was as soothing as the ocean sounds. They stood as they were, keeping their silence while they listened to the tide come in. Arielle wished again that bonnets allowed for easier sidelong glances. She kept her eyes on the sea for as long as she could bear, but then she had to look up. Lord Patrick was watching her.

"I should take you home," he said. "I've kept you from your reading."

"I don't mind."

As they turned to go back, a creature with dirty, matted fur trotted up to them. It was several times larger than Hessy, standing a little taller than Arielle's knee. It hesitated for a moment a few steps away before approaching her. She let go of Lord Patrick's arm and bent down to offer the animal—a dog, her mind supplied—a hand to sniff. The dog licked her glove and whined in a heart wrenching way.

"What a sweet little thing you are," Arielle told it, falling immediately in love with the adoring expression in the dog's dark eyes. "Who do you belong to?"

"Judging by her condition, she's a stray," Lord Patrick said. "If she does have an owner, they've neglected her terribly."

"Then you'll have to come home with me." Arielle hoped Aunt Prissy wouldn't mind adding a dog to the family. She couldn't leave the sweet thing out here on its own. The animal needed a bath and several good meals. And a name. "I shall call you Bingley."

The dog jumped to brace her filthy front paws on Arielle's knees and barked happily.

Arielle giggled. "You like it?"

"Bingley?" Lord Patrick's expression when she looked up at him was difficult to read, but amusement was primary.

"I probably shouldn't name a female dog after a male character, but she's so happy and friendly, just like Mr. Bingley." Arielle shrugged. The dog jumped on her again, trying to get near enough to lick her face and almost toppled her to the ground. Lord Patrick put out a hand to steady her as she laughed. "I dare you to find a more fitting name."

"Impossible," he agreed with a smile. "She's already taken to it and you. I've never seen anyone make friends with an animal so quickly."

Arielle blushed. What was it about compliments from Lord Patrick that discomposed her so? She turned her head away so that her bonnet hid her face. Bingley was wagging her tail so hard that her entire body wiggled, which distracted Arielle and brought on another fit of laughter.

Lord Patrick joined in with a chuckle. "All right, let's get you home."

Bingley seemed content to trot at Arielle's heels, and they soon returned to the Farleys' house. Arielle thanked Lord Patrick again for walking her home, then took the dog around to the back of the house, where she begged a large tub of water from Mrs. Little. Mary helped her get Bingley into the water, and between the two of them, they got the dog clean. Both girls were half drenched by the time they were finished, but Bingley looked like a whole new dog. Now that all the mud had been removed from her long, silky fur, Arielle could see that Bingley was mostly black, with reddish brown on her face and legs.

"You are a beautiful girl," she murmured as she toweled Bingley off and Mary dumped the tub and set it aside to dry. "Do you know what kind of dog she is?"

"Gordon setter," Mary said. "My father used to work for a

gentleman who had a kennel full of hunting dogs." She gave Bingley a pat on the head. The dog responded by licking her fingers. "You do have a way with animals, Miss Arielle. I like it."

Arielle grinned at the girl. "Hopefully Aunt Prissy and Livvie like it too, because I don't think I can give Bingley up."

# Chapter 14

Arielle's guardians willingly welcomed the new addition to the house, especially after she told them about the condition she'd found Bingley in. A small, soft rug was moved from the family parlor to Arielle's room for Bingley to sleep on. Arielle was a little worried about how Hessy would react to the newcomer, but the cat merely turned up his nose and hopped onto the bed.

Arielle went shopping with Aunt Prissy the next day, and as they returned along the Steine, she saw the Duke of Marsham and his mother leaving the Gouldings' house. The now familiar ache hit Arielle, but it was weaker this time, and she carried on her conversation with Aunt Prissy about bonnet ribbons without any outward sign of distress. And she forgot all about it when she was greeted at the door by an overjoyed Bingley.

She heard more about the dowager duchess's visit the following morning from Letitia Goulding, who called to ask Arielle to walk with her.

"She's been so kind to me," Letitia said as they strolled along Marine Parade. "I would have expected her to be conceited and petty, between her title and fortune and how well she's retained her beauty. But she isn't at all—she talks to me as if she thinks I have something worthwhile to say."

## CHAPTER 14

"That shows good sense," Arielle said, "because you do."

Letitia threw her arm around Arielle's shoulders and squeezed. "I knew I'd like you the moment I saw you. I'm sure the duchess will too, and you're bound to like her."

Arielle turned her head away to hide her confusion. Marsham was pursuing the obvious path of courting Letitia, and though thinking of it still caused a tightness in her chest, she couldn't blame him in the least. As that was the case, there was no reason the dowager duchess should notice Arielle, and no call for Arielle to form an opinion about Her Grace. The only future interactions Arielle could foresee were as she kept up her friendship with Letitia once the girl had married the duke.

Letitia had prattled on without waiting for a response, outlining a plan for a picnic on Friday. They would drive a short way to where the white cliffs rose and spend the day eating and walking along the cliff tops. Arielle hadn't been to the cliffs, and she admitted that a picnic there sounded pleasant. But she hadn't been in company with Marsham since the fateful evening at the Gouldings', and she wasn't sure how she'd handle seeing him and Letitia together. Letitia wouldn't hear any demur, however, and by the time they returned to Aunt Prissy's house, Arielle had accepted its inevitability.

\*\*\*

It was just Michael's luck that the weather would be fine for every outing he planned, Patrick thought. The castle, the picnic… Sunny and warm with the right amount of breeze. The rain of the evening before had cleared out, leaving the world fresh and glittering. Even the elements seemed to bend to the Duke of Marsham's whim.

And the location couldn't have been chosen better. The blankets were set up a good way from the cliff top in a green field with a view for miles, the crash of waves below making a calm background music. Servants set out an array of food while the picnickers explored and stretched their legs.

Patrick wasn't complaining. He'd driven Miss Farley and Arielle—and Bingley, who had obediently lain on the floor of the carriage by Arielle's feet for the entire ride—in his landau again, and they had filled the time with cheerful talk. Lady Priscilla had apparently decided to pursue her usual sea-bathing rather than spending the day in the sun, and it seemed that there had been quite a long debate over what bonnet Arielle ought to wear, balancing the need to shade her face against trim that would match her walking dress.

"I still don't see why Aunt Prissy put up such a fuss about you wearing those two colors together," Miss Farley had said. "The bigger bonnet is obviously the right choice when you have a propensity to freckle."

Patrick had glanced back at them, surprised—he'd never noticed Arielle having freckles. She'd caught his look and rolled her eyes. "It was much ado about nothing," she'd said.

Once out of the carriage, Miss Goulding had latched on to Arielle and taken her off to look for wildflowers, while Bingley ran about through the wild grasses, sniffing and exploring. Patrick had taken a moment to note that while Arielle's dress was the light blue of the sky, the ribbons on her bonnet were a darker turquoise. He laughed to himself. Lady Priscilla was right; most fashionable young ladies wouldn't be caught dead wearing a bonnet with contrasting ribbons. But he agreed with Arielle's assessment, that such a fuss was pointless. A hat was a hat, and mismatched ribbons didn't detract from her beauty a jot.

While the others explored the meadow or wandered about, Patrick walked to the cliff edge and looked over. To the left, he could see the line of white chalk cliffs standing stark between the gray water and the blue sky. White, foamy caps topped the waves that rolled in. Gulls cried and wheeled overhead.

He stood smiling, lost in thought, remembering walking with Arielle along Marine Parade. Her willingness to engage him on the subject of history warmed him even now. The delicious sensation of having her full attention might have made him talk longer than he would have otherwise, but she didn't seem to mind. He'd enjoyed discussing books with her and watching her delight and wonder over something as mundane as a stray dog. He admired her ability to befriend Bingley—whom he'd guessed to be a setter but couldn't have predicted what color through all the caked dirt—and he remembered that she'd done the same with his horses. The way animals instantly loved her was yet another thing that intrigued him about her.

But his favorite moments from that day were the ones spent at the end of Marine Parade looking out at the sea. She'd seemed more relaxed there than he'd ever seen her, comfortable with him and the world. He wanted to walk with her here, to see if she loved this view as much as he did.

He was recalled by laughing voices passing him, and he turned. Everyone was moving toward the picnic blankets. The large group divided themselves between two blankets. Patrick tried to get a place beside Arielle, but she was sandwiched between two ladies. He sighed and took an open space, comforting himself that at least Michael wasn't seated near her, either. As soon as he'd finished, Patrick got up and stood nearby, needing space. Arielle was just as crowded, but she didn't seem to mind having Letitia close on one side and Mrs. Ingersoll on the other. The ladies were teasing Arielle good-naturedly about her ribbons. She laughed and told them to take it up with Miss Farley, who had insisted that she wear the bonnet with the wider brim. Mrs. Ingersoll moved to the other blanket, where Miss Farley sat with Mrs. Goulding and two other chaperones, to do just that. Patrick stepped toward the gap she'd left, trying not to appear overeager but desperate to be near Arielle. Before he could get halfway there, however, Lord Preston had slid over. Patrick pressed his lips together. He couldn't blame the earl for wanting more room, but he didn't like that the man's first action after moving was to lean toward Arielle and ask her a question. It wasn't the place or time for a private conversation, however, and Miss Goulding soon called Arielle's attention away.

The group ate and talked and laughed. The gentlemen spoke of races they'd seen and horses they'd backed; the ladies discussed last night's ball and the latest *on dit* from town. Arielle chatted and laughed along with them, and Patrick couldn't help watching her more than the others. Despite her happy smile, her laughter was subdued, and her eyes kept darting to Michael and away. Faint color rose in her cheeks as she did this. Patrick's heart ached; she must know that his brother had chosen her friend. To be here with them could only be painful, and he wished he could offer her some comfort. He felt mildly better when he saw Bingley insert herself into the space between Arielle and Preston to rest her head on her mistress's lap. Arielle stroked the dog's head absently, her expression relaxing almost imperceptibly.

Patrick moved over to join the group on the other blanket for a while, hoping that distance and distraction would ease the ache he felt for Arielle. It didn't. From here he couldn't see her face or hear their conversation, but that only made him think more about her and wonder if she was enjoying herself at all.

After a while he moved back, and his quick observations spoke for themselves. Arielle had fallen silent. Her smile was still firmly fixed in place, but she wasn't laughing anymore, and her aquamarine eyes had gone glassy and distant. This was such a marked change from her usual bright, clear, curious gaze, as if she were drinking in the newness of the world around her, that he was amazed no one else had noticed. Her dog was now sprawled half across her legs, snuggling closer like a furry lap blanket. Judging by how Bingley occasionally licked the inside of Arielle's elbow and kept her adoring gaze fixed on her face, the dog could sense something was off and didn't know what to do about it. Lord Patrick had seen this glazed look from Arielle before, at the Lewes Inn and again at Michael's card party. It was a sign of overwhelm, of emotional exhaustion. The poor girl needed a break.

That was one thing Patrick could do: he could give her a way out.

He rounded the blanket and crouched near her. "Miss Arielle, Miss Farley needs you a moment."

Arielle nodded, her eyes clearing just a bit as she excused herself, slid Bingley gently to the ground, and let Patrick help her to her feet. Bingley jumped up and bounced around them as soon as they were away from the blanket. Halfway to the other group, Patrick leaned over and murmured, "I have a confession to make."

Arielle looked up at him, surprised. He was close enough to her now that he could see the lightest dusting of freckles across her nose, and it made her more adorable than ever. "What could you possibly have to confess?"

"I'm afraid Miss Farley doesn't know yet that she needs you."

"You mean she didn't send you to me?"

Patrick shook his head.

"Then why…?"

"You looked like you needed to get away for a bit."

Arielle blinked at him, then a slow smile spread across her face. "I did. Thank you. Do you mind waiting for me while I speak to Livvie for a moment?"

"Nothing could make me happier."

Arielle grinned at him, probably assuming he was teasing, but he was telling the absolute truth.

She went to kneel beside Miss Farley and spoke in an undertone. He didn't catch the first part of what she said, but he heard, "…walk with Lord Patrick?"

"Of course you may, dear, just stay within sight," Miss Farley said. She looked at him over Arielle's shoulder and her smile quirked a bit wider.

Arielle rose and joined him again. "Will you walk with me?"

"Gladly. I think you'll like the view from the cliff. Shall we?" He offered his arm, and she took it. The warmth of her hand somehow glowed through her glove and his coat. His stomach soared to have her so near. A motion across the other blanket caught his eye: Michael was looking straight at them. The duke raised a single imperious brow, holding Patrick's eye, then sighed and gave the tiniest nod. Patrick glared at his brother—*I don't need your permission*—then turned his back on the group and walked away with Arielle.

They strolled along in silence but for the gentle admonishment Arielle gave Bingley to stay back from the edge. The dog obeyed, astonishing Patrick by turning back to sniff the path farther from the cliff. Was this some kind of magic? Or did animals simply worship Arielle so fully that they'd do whatever she asked to make her happy? Patrick felt a little unsettled that he had so much in common with a dog.

As they stepped up to the cliff edge to look over, Patrick wished that Arielle had chosen a bonnet without such a wide brim so he could see her reaction. She gasped.

"I know those cliffs," she said softly.

Patrick let out the breath he'd been holding. That wasn't a reaction he'd been expecting.

"I haven't seen them from this direction, but I *know* them…"

Arielle rarely spoke about her missing memories, and Patrick had never quite dared to ask. He knew that she'd been washed ashore, and he imagined that anything she remembered might be painful. He didn't want to say something that would make her uncomfortable. Had she been on board a ship in the channel that had wrecked? But where had the rest of the ship gone? Nothing else had washed up in the weeks before or since.

He waited, silently observing the water and the cliffs, hoping she'd say more but equally willing to let her be still.

Eventually, in a quiet voice, she changed the subject. "You must think I'm weak."

Patrick was taken aback. "Why should you think such a thing?" He turned so that he could face her more directly.

"Why wouldn't you?" Her cheeks were flushed. "I'm obviously more fragile than everyone else. I can't even stand an afternoon picnic without needing to get away."

"You are not weak, Miss Arielle. You are, in fact, incredibly brave, surrounded by so much that is new to you." She tilted her head to look at him in disbelief, and he could again see the freckles sprinkled across her nose. A wish surfaced to kiss those freckles—and the full pink lips below—but he shoved the impossible dream back down. "I'm quite serious. You have nothing to be ashamed of. I don't like large groups either, but my position is easier, as I can come and go as I please." He glanced back at the gathering still clustered around the blankets and the servants now serving pastries.

They turned and began to walk along the cliff, staying a safe distance from the edge. "If I may ask," he ventured, "you don't seem bothered by the crowded balls. Why not?"

"I love dancing." Arielle smiled up at him. "I've always loved music, I think, and since I have no musical skill, dancing is my favorite way to enjoy it." She thought a moment. "With so many people in the ballroom that I don't know, they're somehow easier to ignore. I can focus solely on my current partner. But even so, I usually sleep half the next day."

Since she wasn't able to recover this morning from the ball last night, Patrick was even less surprised that she had needed to get away from the others.

"You'll be relieved when the season ends in a few weeks and Brighton empties, I suppose? There will be no balls—but also no crowds—until next summer." At her startled look, he added, "Don't worry—the libraries will stay open."

She laughed, but it wasn't the carefree sound he'd heard from her before. "That *is* a relief." A silence, then, with her head tilted away so he couldn't see her face, she said, "You'll think me silly, but I guess I assumed that most people just... well, *lived* here."

"Lady Priscilla does. But half of us only come for the summer."

## CHAPTER 14

"Where do you all go when you leave Brighton?"

Patrick watched a gull circle and dive for something down below. "Michael spends the latter part of the year in the country on one of his estates before going to London for the winter and spring. Our brother Frederick lives in London year round, and I stay with him when I'm obliged to go to town on business, but I have a house near Hadlow in Kent."

"Will you tell me about it? Is it like the houses here in Brighton?"

Patrick unconsciously stood a little taller. Arielle was naturally curious about everything, but he relished having her interest turned in his direction—not just in what he was saying, but in him and his life.

"It's not much like Brighton houses," he said. "It's bigger, and it stands alone in a grove of elm trees." He pictured the house as he described it—grayish brick, glazed windows, an orderly kitchen garden. A stream ran nearby with a good fishing spot about a two-mile walk away. Smaller than the least of Michael's estates, but comfortable and secluded. Peaceful.

As he spoke, he hoped that Arielle could picture the scene and that she liked it. Not for his sake, or for any deluded wish that she'd want to make his home her own. No, Arielle's affection still belonged to Michael, but Patrick craved her good opinion. Just like Bingley.

"It sounds like a sweet house," she said when he was done. "Like something out of Jane Austen."

Patrick grinned. From anyone else, that would have been faint praise, but he knew how much Arielle loved Miss Austen's works. He took the compliment for what it was.

By now the rest of the party was dividing into pairs and trios to walk along the cliff or the downs. Miss Farley joined them.

"You've had a long enough tête-à-tête for today," she said brightly. "Are you feeling better, Ari?"

"Much." Arielle smiled up at Patrick. "Thank you again, both for noticing I'd had enough and not judging me for it."

"It was my pleasure. Truth be told, rescuing you spared me as well."

\*\*\*

By the time they'd returned to Brighton and Lord Patrick had left them at Lady Priscilla's house, Arielle was exhausted. But Aunt Prissy was waiting for them in the parlor with tea, so she changed and joined the Farleys to talk about the afternoon.

"Did you have a nice time, Ari, dear?" Aunt Prissy asked.

"I did." And it was true. She'd been uncomfortable at first around the Duke of Marsham, particularly with Letitia right there. He'd shown Arielle none of the special attention he'd given her previously. This was embarrassing in itself, because she felt now that she must have read into his earlier behavior too much in thinking he might like her, and she worried that her own infatuation had been too visible.

She'd had to contend with all those thoughts and feelings while participating in the lively conversation. Everyone talked over each other, and nobody listened for more than a moment, each trying to say the wittiest thing and cause the next round of raucous laughter. It would have been too much after a while on a normal day, but on a day when she was trying to bury all her feelings….

Arielle hadn't realized that she'd given any sign that she wished to be anywhere but there. No one else had seemed to notice a change. Only Lord Patrick.

His awareness and concern sent warmth through her. That he would truly *see* her and notice when something was wrong made her stomach do something oddly fluttery. And he'd known exactly what to do to help her, without making her feel badly about it. Lord Patrick had turned an awkward, uncomfortable afternoon into one of the pleasantest she'd had.

"Ari took a nice long walk along the cliffs with Lord Patrick," Olivia informed Aunt Prissy with pretended nonchalance and a poorly suppressed smile.

"I see." Aunt Prissy's face crinkled. "Lord Patrick is a dear. And what did you think of the cliffs, Ari?"

Arielle loved her guardian's wrinkled smile, but she wasn't sure she liked the direction of their suggestions. There was nothing between her and Lord Patrick, nothing but friendship. She seized on Aunt Prissy's question.

"I *remembered* them."

Lady Priscilla and Olivia both gasped and peppered her with questions, which was the change of subject Arielle had hoped for.

"I don't know when I've seen them or from where," she said. "I don't think I've seen them from the cliff top before, but that white rock is too distinct not to be the same."

"So you think you've seen them from the sea?" Olivia asked.

Arielle nodded slowly. "I must have." She closed her eyes and imagined what the looming chalky cliffs would look like if viewed from below. She caught her breath. "Yes. That's it."

She opened her eyes and found both of her friends staring at her. Olivia's eyes were wide. Aunt Prissy looked thoughtful but unsurprised.

"That would make sense," the older woman said. "You were washed up on shore, which would mean you'd been at sea. You must have seen the cliffs from whatever boat you'd been on."

Olivia nodded, but Arielle wasn't sure. She'd seen boats on the water and moored at the docks, but they hadn't sparked any recognition—not for any boat in particular, and not for sea-faring craft in general. She kept this to herself, however. A boating accident would be the most logical explanation, and she couldn't come up with anything equally plausible.

## Chapter 15

The next morning, Arielle was called from her reading by the arrival of a visitor: the Dowager Duchess of Marsham. Arielle had met her at the Gouldings' dinner and had thought her a grand and stately lady, not so much older than Olivia but without Livvie's carefree lightness. Given the direction of the duke's attentions, however, Arielle couldn't understand why she'd be visiting them in Marine Parade, nor why she'd be studying Arielle with such a sharp eye.

Olivia had gone to the library with Lindsay, so Arielle and Lady Priscilla welcomed their guest alone and offered her tea. After briefly greeting Her Grace, who offered her hand for a sniff and a lick, Bingley lay at Arielle's feet, content to be nearby.

While they waited for the tea things to arrive, Her Grace questioned Arielle. By now she was used to the inquisition—every new acquaintance above a certain age had done the same thing. But Arielle had to give the duchess credit: she satisfied her curiosity with much more class than the rest.

"You read beautifully at the Gouldings' dinner," Her Grace said, smiling disarmingly. "Do you enjoy reading?"

"Very much," Arielle said. "If left to myself, I'd likely forget everything else and read all day without noticing the time."

The dimples in the corners of the duchess's mouth deepened. "I've known one or two people who have done just that."

"Really? I've thought I was alone—no one I know has ever admitted to it."

She laughed. "Oh, yes. My husband used to read for hours, God rest him, and when Patrick was a boy, he'd sneak out of the house before lessons and return just in time for dinner with the book he'd just finished."

Arielle just managed to stop her mouth from falling open. She'd known Lord Patrick liked reading—they'd talked about books, and he'd read some of the same ones she had—but she'd never have guessed that he would ignore his duty in order to read. Perhaps he'd outgrown the impulse.

"Have you other accomplishments?" the duchess asked. "Besides dancing, which, likewise, you do quite well."

"I'm afraid not, Your Grace," Arielle said. She'd expected the admission to be more mortifying when made to such a person, but she felt no judgement. "I've half made up my mind to ask Letitia Goulding to teach me magic, though, after her performance."

"She was remarkable," Her Grace agreed. "But accomplishments are overrated, as I'm sure your guardians have told you." Here she flashed Aunt Prissy a wry smile. Aunt Prissy grinned back, her face crinkling like an old apple. "Do you know how to keep house?"

"A bit," Arielle said. "Olivia and Mrs. Little have been teaching me." Her lessons with the cook had consisted more of how to make a pie crust or dough for sweet rolls than how to plan a dinner menu, but she didn't mention this. She wasn't sure if baking was an accomplishment the dowager duchess would think suitable for a lady. She took a deep breath. "It's probably simpler, Your Grace, to assume I don't have any skills or knowledge rather than asking about one at a time. I don't remember my life before coming here, but I can't have experienced much, because everything has seemed so very new to me."

The Dowager Duchess of Marsham considered her thoughtfully. "You're no worse off than half of the young ladies making their debut in town each season," she said finally. "Better, in fact, because while so many of them are empty-headed widgeons, you seem quite intelligent and capable of learning."

"She is," Aunt Prissy agreed, with a smile at Arielle. "Perhaps we could be more diligent in her education, but we've been enjoying the season and these first weeks together. I daresay, life before Ari came now seems dreadfully dull, and I don't know how we bore it."

Arielle blushed. She was spared answering by the arrival of the tea tray. The topic shifted then to Brighton and changes that had been seen in the town in the last few years. Aunt Prissy, apparently, had lived there for the last twenty years, and the duchess had been coming for the summers for nearly as long.

"It's a shame that Prinny isn't here," the duchess said. "I'm sure Miss Arielle and her friends would have liked to attend a concert at the Pavilion. Have you seen inside it?" Arielle shook her head. "It's lavishly fitted up in the Oriental style. A bit obtrusive for my taste—too much red and gold—but I've never seen anything like it."

"Too many dragons," Aunt Prissy agreed. "He came down for a week in June, before Ari arrived. I'd thought he'd be back, but he seems to have found other occupations this year."

They chatted on. Arielle began to relax now that the conversation didn't center on her. She liked the Dowager Duchess; Letitia's prediction had been accurate. At last the duchess set down her teacup and thanked Lady Priscilla for her hospitality.

"I've had a lovely time," she said. "I look forward to seeing more of you, Miss Arielle."

Aunt Prissy and Arielle walked with her to the door. When she was gone, Arielle said softly, "She was very kind, but I can't think why she would show such interest in me. She seemed like she had a reason to ask her questions, beyond nosy curiosity."

"Can't you?" Lady Priscilla's eyebrows arched up.

Arielle blushed. "Two weeks ago I might have thought it was because His Grace was… attentive, but we all know that he'll marry Letitia."

"She has another eligible son, you know, who has been even more attentive."

"You can't mean—"

But Aunt Prissy just raised one shoulder and glided off toward the stairs.

Arielle stared after her. The Farleys' teasing smiles about Lord Patrick yesterday had been one thing; suggesting that Her Grace had come to interrogate her youngest son's potential bride was quite another. Lord Patrick didn't think of her like that… did he? He'd never given her any sign of particular regard. Had she missed it? Surely, Aunt Prissy was simply engaging in wishful thinking. It wasn't an unpleasant notion—Lord Patrick was one of the best men she knew—but it wouldn't do to make a big deal over an old lady's flight of fancy. She did need to find her true love, a prospect that worried her more since learning that everyone would be leaving Brighton for the winter, but with Marsham she'd let her hopes carry her away in a fruitless infatuation, and she wouldn't make that mistake again. She refused to read into every interaction or trust appearances of affection. It was better to put it from her mind until she had something more concrete to hold onto.

# Chapter 16

After three days of rain, which Arielle spent with Olivia and Lady Priscilla, having some of those housekeeping lessons that their social schedule had previously precluded, the sky finally cleared. Letitia Goulding sent a note inviting Arielle to go out on a pleasure boat that afternoon. Letitia declared that if she spent another moment indoors with no one but her mother for company, she would combust. Arielle had been content to stay home, and she always enjoyed the Farleys' company, but she had to own that she was ready to have a break from lessons about planning dinner parties and proper invitation etiquette. She was curious about the boats, especially after Aunt Prissy's guess about where she had come from. She wanted to see if she could gain any flashes of insight by being aboard one.

When she went to the docks, Arielle found that a large party was gathering. She ought to have expected it. Letitia enjoyed being surrounded by a crowd of friends as much as Marsham. To Arielle's relief, only four could fit in a boat with the crew. Four was a small enough group for her to be comfortable. The party divided. Arielle was shunted, to her mild dismay, aboard a boat with Letitia and the duke. She'd hoped to end up in the other boat with Lord Patrick, away from Marsham, and had thought he'd been reaching out to hand her aboard. But between Letitia taking her arm and everyone jostling each other in their eagerness, she found herself sitting instead beside Mr. Sharpton. The gentleman promptly began telling her of all the yachts he'd been on and the sailing races he'd won. Arielle smiled and nodded politely while thinking to herself that he was a poor distraction from the flirting couple beside them. Why couldn't she have been on the other boat? Lord Preston, Miss Crewe, and Miss Rowles were the rest of Lord Patrick's quartet. She thought she caught an unguarded, jealous look from Lord Patrick as the boats pulled away from the dock, as if he was as annoyed by the way the group had divided as she was.

Arielle didn't have much attention to spare, however. The motion of the boat made her uneasy, and she clung to her seat with both hands. She was soon confident of one thing: she'd never been on a boat, and she did not wish to ever again. The waves were choppy after all the rain, and the wind gusted restlessly. Even so, the sea was beautiful, and the shoreline behind them soon spread out in a wide panorama with the white cliffs just visible in the distance. Arielle looked about in awe.

They'd been out for less than an hour when something bobbing in the waves caught Arielle's eye. "What's that?"

She'd interrupted Mr. Sharpton mid sentence. Flustered, he recovered himself and tried to see where she was looking. "What's what?"

She pointed. It looked like a head, like someone swimming, but then it disappeared below the waves. A moment later, it reappeared closer to the boat. "A seal!"

"They're often seen around these parts. That's where the

legend of the selkies comes from."

And Mr. Sharpton was off again, describing the women who could take off their seal skins to live among humans for a short while before needing to return to the sea. If anyone else had been telling the story, Arielle would have found it fascinating, but as it was, she wished he would stop talking. She leaned on the boat's railing watching the seal frolic in the water a few yards from the boat. Another seal's head emerged a moment later. They barked as they played, and Arielle laughed. A third gray head joined them, but this was different—a dolphin's long nose and chittering cry made Arielle lean farther over the railing. The creatures were as happy as Bingley, and she delighted to watch them, forgetting her companions for a joyful moment.

As if from a distance, she heard voices calling to her.

"Miss Arielle, I beg you get away from the side."

"Ari, do sit down before you fall!"

She shook her head, half turning to tell them that she was fine. She'd no more than opened her mouth to say the words before something big slammed into the bottom of the boat. The craft jerked sideways, and Arielle toppled over into the frigid water.

It was the strangest thing. Terror had filled her for the split second between railing and waves, but as soon as Arielle had sunk beneath the surface, she felt peaceful. She opened her eyes and saw the sunlight dancing as if through crystal. The water caressed her skin. She'd lost her bonnet in the fall, and now her hair came partially loose from its pins, flowing free. This felt good. This felt *right*. She belonged here with the dolphin and seals and—was that an orca that had bumped the boat?

## CHAPTER 16

Arielle surrendered to these sensations—new, but also familiar—for about five seconds before her lungs began to suggest that she breathe. She tried to swim upward, but her skirt weighed her down and tangled her legs so that she could barely kick. Her new animal friends circled in confusion and dismay. The peace she'd felt was replaced by fear. Her lungs screamed for air as she struggled in vain to reach the surface.

***

Patrick was jealous. After Michael's promises to leave Arielle to herself, the duke had somehow still contrived to have her in his boat. Was Letitia Goulding not enough? Must he claim Arielle too? Or was this that opportunistic cad Sharpton's doing? Patrick had never liked the man and now found his animosity growing.

Patrick had shot dozens of disgruntled looks toward his brother's boat during the past hour. So he was watching when swimming shapes approached Arielle's side and saw her lean over the railing. Could there be a worse time for her uncanny affinity for animals?

"Pull her back," he muttered under his breath. "Keep her safe, you fools."

He saw something jerk their boat, saw everyone tossed about. Saw Arielle flung over the edge and into the water.

His heart leapt into his throat. Only vaguely aware of the commotion in the other boat, Patrick tore off his boots and coat without taking his eyes off the point where she'd fallen. Within seconds, he was diving overboard.

The water closed in over him, familiar and comfortable. He'd never been more thankful that his father had taught them all to swim as children. He could see her struggling, kicking against her entangling skirts, her hair loose and wrapping around her face as she fought. He forced his way downward to her. Gray shapes circled as if confused and helpless. Two seals and a dolphin scattered as he approached, and a larger, darker shape just visible in the distance vanished as well. His racing heart skipped a beat as her movements slowed. His own lungs burned as he grabbed for her wrist and tugged her upward, pulling her closer, sliding his arm beneath her shoulders.

Their heads broke the surface, and he sucked in air, letting it out in a laugh of relief as Arielle gasped, sputtered, and coughed beside him. Her eyes were wide and frightened, and his arm tightened around her as he treaded water.

"You're safe," he murmured to her, panting from the exertion. "I won't let you go."

One of her arms came around his shoulders, and she used the other to try to help swim. Michael's boat was nearest, and eager hands reached down to lift Arielle back in.

"Get her back to shore directly," Patrick called. "We'll follow you."

He swam back to the other boat, where alarmed and admiring cries greeted him. Preston commended his quick thinking, admitting that he himself couldn't swim. Patrick just nodded, trying to control the shaking. He may have told Arielle that finding Michael washed up on the beach had been his most terrifying moment, but today it had been surpassed.

They drew up alongside the dock, and everyone disembarked. Arielle was already on the beach, surrounded by Miss Goulding, Michael, and Sharpton. Miss Farley, skirts lifted and hat askew, was running down the beach toward them. One of the sailors was jogging along beside, obviously sent on an

## CHAPTER 16

errand to bring her.

The group made way for Miss Farley, allowing her to pull Arielle into a tight hug. Patrick watched as she held the girl at arm's length and tutted over the state of her before hugging her again. Miss Goulding was now in tears. Michael drew her aside to comfort her, with Miss Crewe hovering nearby to help.

Patrick dropped his boots and coat on the dock and stood dripping. A servant—the Farleys' footman—hurried down the beach with an armful of blankets. Patrick met him and took one. He unfolded it and turned to Arielle.

\*\*\*

Arielle took Olivia's hands. "I'm fine, Livvie, really. Just… just shaken. And wet."

"James is bringing blankets. What happened?"

"Something bumped us," Arielle said, afraid that if she mentioned the orca her guardian would worry even more. "Is Letitia all right? I think she's taking this all worse than I am. Can you check on her for me?"

Olivia was none too keen to leave Arielle's side, she could tell, but the woman obliged. Arielle took the moment to breathe. She'd been fussed over since she'd been pulled back into the boat, and she needed space. Her gaze fell on the sea, and she wondered at the animals' behavior and the strange familiarity she'd felt.

Warm hands draped a blanket around her, lingering a breath or two longer on her shoulders.

"I thought I warned you not to swim on that part of the beach."

Lord Patrick's low voice sent shivers down Arielle's spine. She turned to smile at him. His shirt clung wetly, and she had to force herself not to study the muscular planes of his chest and shoulders. His light brown hair hung heavy and dripping over his forehead, and his gray eyes were deeper and darker than she remembered. For a dizzying moment, she wanted nothing more than to throw herself into his arms. She'd felt so safe with him supporting her in the water. To have those strong arms come around her and hold her…

She shook herself. It was the shock causing this reaction, nothing more. He'd rescued her; it was only natural that she, in her current condition, would want to cling to his strength. She hugged the blanket tighter around herself.

"I… er… thank you," she said feebly. "You risked your life to save mine."

"I'd hardly call it risking my life," he said, his mouth curling up at one corner. "I know how to swim."

"But you dove in after me. That was very brave."

He had not stepped back after giving her the blanket. He was close, so close that she could watch a drop of water trickle down his temple and along his jaw. She wanted to reach out and wipe it away. She clenched her fists in the warm wool of the blanket. His eyes held hers intently.

"I couldn't have done anything else, Miss Arielle."

She believed him. In that moment, she believed he'd have done whatever it took, even draining the sea to save her, if that's what had been necessary. Her stomach erupted into flutters.

"I—I'll never forget it," she whispered.

For a second Lord Patrick looked like he might close the distance between them, and Arielle shivered with nerves and anticipation. But Olivia bustled over to interrupt them. She handed Lord Patrick a blanket and put an arm around Arielle.

"You're shivering, dear! Let's get you home and into dry things." She smiled at Arielle's rescuer. "I don't know how to thank you, Lord Patrick. Please come by anytime for tea—I know Aunt Prissy and I would love to hear your side of the story. But you ought to go get dried off as well."

Lord Patrick bowed and assured her that it was his pleasure to be of assistance. He wrapped the blanket around his shoulders, gave Arielle one last heart-stopping look, and turned to join his brother. Arielle couldn't help watching after him wistfully, wondering what would have happened if they'd been given just one more minute alone.

She went along with Olivia and allowed herself to be fussed over some more. She had a hot bath and clean dry clothes, and then Aunt Prissy insisted on tucking her into bed with extra covers. Bingley whined from her rug on the floor until Arielle gave in and patted the bed in invitation. Hessy wasn't impressed when he jumped up to find Bingley already lying close against Arielle's side, but he made a new place for himself in the gap between Arielle's shoulder and cheek. The two of them warmed Arielle better than the bath had. Aunt Prissy had left her with a book, but she couldn't concentrate on reading.

Animals liked her, and she liked them. She'd known this—the two furry bodies snuggling with her were proof. But this afternoon had been different. She hadn't needed the little voice in her mind to tell her what the creatures were. She recognized them—not those individuals, perhaps, but she knew she'd seen seals, dolphins, and orcas before. But how could that be? How was it that she knew *them*, but cats, dogs, and horses, animals that were common in Brighton, were entirely new to her?

Where had she come from, and what kind of magic held her memories at bay?

And what on earth had happened between her and Lord Patrick? Was Aunt Prissy right—did he have feelings for Arielle? Her earlier attempts to dismiss it as wishful fancy on her guardian's part fell flat when she remembered the way he'd looked at her on the beach. And what about her—what did *she* feel? It was true she'd decided that she hadn't been really in love with Marsham, and she could be around him and Letitia without feeling anything more uncomfortable than awkwardness. She liked and respected Lord Patrick. They had a lot in common, and he understood her better than almost anyone. But then today, when he'd pulled her to the surface... If it hadn't been for the fact that he was keeping them both afloat, she would have flung her arms around his neck in relief. She'd felt so safe with him, despite the lingering traces of fear she'd seen in his eyes.

If all this was true, was it possible that her feelings at the beach, her overwhelming desire to be held by him, were a symptom of love? Did she love Lord Patrick? Or was she still rattled by her brush with death? And if she loved him, was it true and lasting love, or would it fade the way her infatuation with Marsham had?

Arielle's head spun. Despite the hours she'd spent in bed that afternoon, she remained awake for several hours into the night as well, without gaining a single ounce of clarity.

# Chapter 17

"What the devil, Michael!"

Patrick stormed into his brother's study without knocking. He'd stopped at home for a few minutes to change, catching up to his brother minutes after Michael had walked Miss Goulding to her door and returned home. This conversation couldn't wait.

Michael looked up, brows raised. "What seems to be the problem?"

"You were supposed to stop giving Arielle Farley special attention. She shouldn't have been in your boat!"

Michael held up a hand to stop him. "I had nothing to do with that—it was Letitia's outing, and she wanted to be with her dearest friend. For what it's worth, her plan was for you to be the fourth in our party, before Sharpton butted his way in."

Patrick gritted his teeth. "Why was she even leaning so far out? Why didn't you stop her?"

"We tried." Michael glared at him. "Then something struck the boat. And before you accuse me of anything else, I would have gone in after her, but Letitia fainted, and if I hadn't caught her, she would have gone overboard too. By the time I looked back up, you were already in."

Patrick scowled and paced in front of the desk. He couldn't

shake the sick terror he'd felt when Arielle had gone under. He knew it was unfair to take his feelings out on his brother, but an argument between them had been a long time coming, and it might as well be now.

Michael sighed. "Look, I know we've been at odds ever since Arielle showed up, but I'm done. Believe it or not, I'm quite fond of Letitia. She and I both agree that you're a much better fit for Arielle. Just don't waste too much more time before you declare yourself or Sharpton may do it first."

Patrick sank into a chair, deflated. "She doesn't like him," he said. "But I don't know how much she likes me either."

Michael snorted. "You're a blind fool, you know that? If Arielle Farley had looked at me the way she was looking at you this afternoon, there's a good chance I'd have run off with her and let Frederick have the title."

Patrick glowered at him.

"I said *if*, little brother. My point was that she more than likes you, if I'm any judge."

Patrick shook his head and got up to leave. He wanted to believe she too had experienced the crackling energy and awareness between them at the beach. But how much of that had been panic and relief because she'd just nearly died? And what did Michael know, anyway? Arielle had spent weeks gazing at Michael in a way to make a whole ballroom jealous, and he'd insensibly chosen another woman.

***

Arielle was relieved the next morning when Lindsay came in to help her dress for the day. She'd half expected to be forced to stay abed longer, and she couldn't bear another minute of

## CHAPTER 17

inactivity. She sat patiently still while the abigail pinned up her hair, then hurried down to breakfast. Aunt Prissy and Olivia both smiled up at her from the table.

"How are you feeling, Ari, dear?" Aunt Prissy asked.

"Very well, thank you." Arielle sat and accepted a plate of food from the footman. She ate as eagerly as was polite, but last night's tea had been hours ago, and she'd been so preoccupied that she hadn't eaten much.

"I have a book to return at the library this morning," Olivia said, spreading blackberry jam on a piece of toast. "Would you like to go with me?"

Arielle agreed readily. "I finished my own book too." She didn't remember much of what the last few chapters had said, but it had been an insipid book, so she didn't mind.

The blue sky of the day before was gone, replaced by heavy gray clouds that promised rain later, but Arielle was glad to be out of the house. After they'd exchanged their books, she convinced Olivia to walk a little farther along Marine Parade. Her restlessness wasn't fully appeased, but Olivia insisted that they turn around.

"We don't want to overstrain you after you may have caught a chill."

Arielle sighed but didn't argue.

When they returned to the house, they found a guest waiting with Aunt Prissy. Arielle's heart sped up as she heard his voice through the drawing room door. Her fingers fumbled clumsily with her bonnet ribbons and the buttons of her spencer. Olivia, amused, waited for her so that they could walk in together, with Bingley at her heels.

Lord Patrick rose when they entered and bowed over each of their hands in turn. He glanced up at Arielle's face as he straightened, seeming reluctant to release her hand. Heat rose in her cheeks. She'd questioned whether the feelings of yesterday were a fleeting thing of the moment, but no: she wanted to step closer, to keep hold of his hand, to feel him brush his lips over her fingers. She bit her lip and dropped her gaze, afraid of what he'd see if she met his eyes.

They sat, and Lord Patrick said, "I called this morning to see if you've recovered from your accident yesterday, Miss Arielle."

"I'm quite recovered, thank you." She spoke softly to her hands in her lap.

"We put Ari straight to bed," Olivia said. "One can't be too careful when one has been out in wet clothes. What about you, your lordship? Are you well?"

"Better now that I know Miss Arielle has taken no harm from the adventure."

Arielle flicked a glance at him and found him watching her. Her color rose. She half wished to be alone with him, to resolve together the question of who felt what and how much. But that was only slightly less terrifying than falling into deep water without being able to swim, and she clung to Olivia and Aunt Prissy's presence like a life preserver. Her hand found Bingley's soft ears and scratched behind them.

"Ari hasn't said much about what happened," Olivia went on. "We didn't want to press her after the shock, but we did hope to get a more complete story from you, Lord Patrick."

"I'm afraid I can't tell you more than anyone else," he said. "Miss Arielle was leaning over the railing. Something struck the boat, and she was thrown overboard. I dove in after her." There was a tightness in his voice, as if he didn't care to relive the anxiety of the events. Then his tone softened as he added to

## CHAPTER 17

Arielle, "Why were you leaning so far out? Was there something in the water?"

Arielle wanted to give a vague answer like she'd given Olivia the day before. Up until now, no one had seemed to mind how she was with animals, but yesterday…. She was ashamed of the trouble that gift had caused, to Lord Patrick more than anyone. He had every right to be upset. But he also had a right to know the truth.

"A dolphin and a couple of seals were playing." Could her face burn any brighter? She kept her gaze on Bingley's dark, liquid eyes so she wouldn't have to see disappointment or disapproval from the others. Bingley loved her too much to judge her. "They were… more interesting than my companions in the boat."

Olivia let out a tiny snort of suppressed laughter. At least her fear for Arielle hadn't crushed her sense of humor.

"Did you see what bumped the boat?"

Arielle nodded.

"What was it?"

"An orca." She shrugged, still unwilling to look up. "I think it was trying to play too. It didn't mean any harm."

"Of course not, dear," Aunt Prissy said. "But I hope you'll remember to stay safely away from the sides next time you're on a boat."

"Oh, I have no desire ever to go on another one," Arielle said firmly, remembering the unpleasant rolling motion and her annoyingly chatty companion.

Tea arrived, and Olivia introduced a new topic: the private ball that the Dowager Duchess of Marsham was holding at the beginning of next week. Arielle listened quietly. Had she ever noticed before the pleasant cadence of Lord Patrick's voice?

Why was she suddenly so aware of him in the chair opposite hers, even with her eyes averted?

Her embarrassment was so acute that it was a relief when he left, and yet she was disappointed too. Arielle was so tangled up in questions and emotions that she had to retire to the parlor to be alone with her thoughts under the pretense of starting her new book.

# Chapter 18

By Monday, Patrick was ready for the ball to be over. He'd been as helpful to his mother as possible over the past week of preparing, but he still didn't see why she had to host it at his house rather than Michael's, especially since the whole purpose of the gathering was to announce Michael's betrothal to Miss Goulding. But their mother was convinced that Marine Parade was much better than the Steine, particularly on a moonlit evening if any of their guests wanted to step outside for fresh air.

There would be about forty guests, since his dining room could only squeeze in fifteen couples. Arielle Farley and her guardians would be among them.

Patrick hadn't seen Arielle since his visit the day after the boating incident, and he'd been unable to get her out of his head. He *couldn't* be mistaken about their interaction on the beach—she must have felt something too. But then, why had she been so shy and reserved when he'd called the next morning? She'd barely looked at him once. Was she embarrassed? And if so, what for? He'd hoped, when he called, to receive some kind of encouragement from her, some sign that the affections he longed for might be, in some degree, his. He'd been sorely disappointed. Far from appearing to wish for his attention, Arielle had been more distant than usual, even distracted.

Patrick ran his hands through his hair for the twentieth time. He'd see her tonight. He would dance with her—a waltz, even if to procure it he had to bribe Miss Farley to alter Arielle's dance card—and he'd find out then if she'd welcome his suit.

He left the house soon after breakfast, unable to contain his restlessness and unwilling to face questions about his irritability. He had one of his horses saddled and took a long, aimless ride over the downs, returning in the early afternoon to prepare for the ball. The last few hours dragged by, but at last the guests began to arrive, and Patrick stood in the hall with his mother and brother to receive them.

His heart, already drumming in his ears, sped up when Arielle arrived. He kept his composure with an effort, greeting Lady Priscilla and Miss Farley warmly but without letting his gaze leave Arielle for any length of time. When she reached him, she glanced around the entrance hall.

"I finally made it past the door." Her smile was shy but teasing, recalling her unexpected appearance on his doorstep that first day.

"Perhaps that was my goal in hosting," he said, "since you never took me up on my invitation to come to the door again."

Her cheeks pinked.

"Will you save me a waltz?"

The color in her cheeks brightened, but she nodded. Then she hurried off, biting her lip to control her smile.

Patrick didn't bother to hide his grin. He ignored Michael's knowing smirk and pretended that he didn't see the pull in the corners of his mother's mouth that said she was smothering a laugh. His family could think what they wanted; he was just

## CHAPTER 18

elated to have a waltz with Arielle.

When all the guests had arrived, everyone gathered in the dining room. It was cramped and hot, but soon the guests would spread out. There would be dancing in the cleared-out dining room, thanks to the quartet his mother had hired, and refreshments laid out in the drawing room. Card tables had been set up in the back parlor. But first, the announcement.

Patrick was across the room from Arielle. She was near the window with Lady Priscilla and Miss Farley, and Lord Preston stood nearby, no doubt poised to claim the first dance. Patrick felt a twinge of jealousy, but he didn't wish to trade—the first would be an allemande. A small, makeshift stage had been set up in the corner where the musicians would take their place, but before they did, Patrick's mother stepped up.

She spoke a few words of welcome, then said, "It is also my pleasure to make a joyful announcement this evening. In a month's time, my son, the Duke of Marsham, will wed Miss Letitia Goulding." She beamed and held out her hands. Michael and Miss Goulding each took a hand and joined her on the stage. Applause rang out and congratulations flowed as they stepped down and passed through the crowd, preparing to take their place at the top of the set and leaving the stage free for the musicians to begin.

Patrick had only given half of his attention to his mother: he was watching Arielle. As Michael and his bride-to-be had been announced, the color leached from Arielle's face until she was nearly as white as her gown. Patrick's happiness faded with it, replaced by the familiar pang of disappointment. He'd been a fool to think that she was already over Michael, that she might like *him* instead.

He allowed himself to be swept into the hall by guests who

were uninclined to dance, pressing himself against the wall until they'd dispersed to cards or refreshments. He took a fortifying breath and went back to watch the dancing.

As expected, Arielle was dancing with Preston. Her pale face was still a stark contrast to her vivid hair and eyes. It was a small consolation to Patrick's jealousy that she seemed barely aware of Preston or his attempts at conversation. Patrick noticed that the Farleys, still in their place by the window, were watching with narrowed eyes. So he wasn't the only one concerned by what he saw.

The dance ended. Somehow, instead of returning to Lady Priscilla, Arielle disappeared into the press of people while Preston found himself a more attentive partner. Patrick frowned and wove his way back to the hall. As he emerged from the dining room, the front door closed. Opening it, he saw a figure running across the street and down toward the beach, her white gown glowing ghostly in the moonlight.

"What are you waiting for?" He glanced back and saw Miss Farley in the hall. She hurried over and shot him a meaningful glare. "Go after her."

\*\*\*

Arielle panted to a stop at the edge of the water. She was shaken, more shaken than she'd expected. Letitia's engagement was no surprise, and she honestly rejoiced for her friend at the match. But seeing them on the musicians' platform, they'd looked... different. No, Letitia had looked the same: beautiful, poised, perfect. It was Marsham. She'd been acquainted with him for weeks, so she recognized him, of course, but whatever familiarity, whatever spark of memory she'd felt before was

## CHAPTER 18

gone. It was as if she'd never remembered his face. He was someone apart, unrelated, completely unconnected to her past.

The realization had almost knocked her from her feet. The mysterious connection between Marsham and her past had been tenuous at best, but it had been there. Suddenly, she felt lost, unmoored. She'd lost her only link to whoever she'd been before.

Now only the sea knew where she'd come from, and the waves weren't telling.

*If only I could swim out and discover what secrets you're keeping,* she thought. *How deep would I have to dive to find answers? Would the seals tell me? Or the dolphins? What is the magic that keeps my past at bay?*

Without thinking, she reached down and slid the slipper from one foot and then the other. She stepped forward until the foam lapped around her toes, then up to her ankles. She held her skirt up with one hand so that the salt water wouldn't ruin the white silk.

A voice called behind her. "Miss Arielle!"

Arielle paused and half turned. Lord Patrick was striding across the beach, swiftly covering the distance between them. He stopped with the toes of his boots just barely within reach of the lapping waves.

"What are you doing?" He sounded breathless, though he hadn't been running. "Is your heart so broken that you would end yourself over this?"

Arielle gaped at him. Why would he think that? A cold splash on the backs of her knees startled her, and she looked down. She didn't remember coming out this far. Her skirt was bunched in one silk-gloved hand, just clear of the surf. She walked back toward shore, toward Lord Patrick, letting the fabric fall.

"No," she said. "I'm not—I would never…"

"Then what are you doing here?"

Arielle threw one more look over her shoulder at the dark waves. "I needed air and… answers."

"Answers?"

Lord Patrick's face was in shadow. She suddenly wanted to explain everything—about remembering his brother, about the magic and the deadline, about feeling suddenly adrift. If anyone would listen and at least try to understand, it would be him. But his unreadable gaze made her nervous, and the words spilled out in a confused jumble.

"I knew he couldn't marry me. I did. But he was so… and I was a fool. But… it's just that I *remembered*, and now…" Arielle took a slow, shaky breath. She closed her eyes and saw Marsham as he'd stood on the platform beside Letitia, and again she saw the last fragile thread connecting her to her past snapping and drifting like spider silk. Her lower lip trembled, and she pressed them together hard.

Lord Patrick stepped closer and took her free hand in his. "Don't cry, Ari. Please. Come back in and dance with me." His voice was as soft and gentle as the waves around her bare toes. "Miss Farley is worrying." He reached up to stroke away the single tear that had leaked out.

His use of her nickname sent a delicious shiver through Arielle. He was so close and so sweet, and she wondered what it would be like to kiss him in the moonlight. She opened her mouth to say that she'd rather stay out here and talk to him—she had so much to say, and she'd done such a wretched job of it—but he was right. She couldn't leave Olivia to worry over her.

## CHAPTER 18

She nodded, and he gave her his handkerchief to dry her feet so that she could put her slippers back on. He offered her his arm, and she took it. She pondered how to say what she wanted as they walked back, but there wasn't time, and she didn't want to botch the explanation a second time. Olivia was waiting on the doorstep. When they reached her, she pulled Arielle into a silent hug. She deserved an explanation too, but instead of demanding answers, she led the way back inside. The last strains of a reel reached them as they crossed the hall, and the dancers were taking their places for a waltz.

"Shall we?" murmured Lord Patrick.

Arielle allowed herself to relax into his arms, losing herself in the dance. The room was stuffy and overfull, but somehow everyone else melted away. Even her missing past felt less relevant in the face of this moment, here and now. Lord Patrick didn't take his eyes off her, but he seemed preoccupied, uncertain. She wondered if he was still thinking about what had just happened on the beach. Could she pull him aside to talk to him again? She wanted to smooth the faint furrow from between his brows.

But when the song ended, Arielle was claimed by Mr. Sharpton, who glared at Lord Patrick. Arielle couldn't imagine what Lord Patrick could have done to upset the gentleman, but she deemed it wisest to keep her questions to herself and accept the next dance. She'd have to find another time to talk to Lord Patrick. Soon. Perhaps she could suggest that he call tomorrow morning to walk out with her.

When Marsham asked her to dance, Arielle was so flustered she almost said no. Lord Patrick's agitated words at the beach rang in her mind. He'd thought she was in love with the duke, so in love that she might destroy herself because Marsham was marrying Letitia. How could she dance with the duke now? But she collected herself with an effort. His Grace was a friend, and she didn't want to offend him. And it was only La Boulanger.

"I congratulate you, Your Grace," she said, as the music began. "Letitia is one of my very favorite people, and she'll make an excellent wife."

Marsham grinned, and Arielle remembered how that smile used to make her knees weak. Now it merely reminded her of his brother and called up an answering smile of her own. "I agree most heartily, Miss Arielle. She is magnificent, isn't she?"

"Exemplary."

They teasingly traded superlatives for a few minutes. Then Marsham surprised her. "You're rather remarkable yourself. Has my brother told you that?"

Arielle almost misstepped. Why would he think Lord Patrick had been complimenting her? Was he of the same opinion as Aunt Prissy, that Lord Patrick wanted to court her? "O-ought he to?" she stammered.

"Yes," Marsham said simply. The dance separated them and then brought them back together. "So he didn't say anything of import when the two of you were... not here?"

Arielle's face burned. She hadn't considered how their disappearance would look to others. "Nothing," she said, as lightly as she could. "I... needed air. Lord Patrick and Livvie came outside to accompany me." Unbidden, the memory of Lord Patrick wiping away her tear came to mind, and her breath hitched.

Marsham accepted her excuse with easy grace, but his expression remained thoughtful for the rest of the dance.

## CHAPTER 18

Arielle wanted to talk to Lord Patrick more than ever, but he was already leading Miss Rowles to the floor when she saw him next, and then Arielle was engaged for the dance after that. It wasn't until the music ended and the remaining guests were milling around, talking and eating, that she was able to slip through the crowd to stand beside him.

"Would you—would you call sometime this week and go walking with me?"

He smiled, and the warmth of his expression made her wonder if she'd imagined his earlier preoccupation. "I would be honored, Miss Arielle."

She grinned at him, then wove her way back through the crowd to Olivia and Aunt Prissy. The three of them walked the short way home, and Arielle fell into bed exhausted. Her dreams were filled with dancing and a moonlit beach.

# Chapter 19

Letitia and her mother called the next morning. The two girls settled onto the couch while the three older women talked on the other side of the room.

"Congratulations," Arielle said, taking Letitia's hands. "I'm so happy for you and Marsham both."

Letitia beamed. "He's everything I ever dreamed of and more," she sighed happily. "And I'm sorry you had to hear about it at the ball with everyone else—I wanted to tell you first, but I had to promise most faithfully to keep it a secret."

"Naturally," Arielle agreed. The actual betrothal had been a secret, but no one could say it was a surprise. "I'm not upset at all. The two of you deserve each other, and it's only been a question of when he would ask you. When *did* he ask?"

"Last week. He took me for a drive in his phaeton, over the downs, you know, and he stopped where there was a splendid view, and he turned to me and asked me to make him the happiest man alive. And of course I said yes, as soon as I could talk again, because he quite took my breath away."

Letitia's entire countenance glowed, and Arielle couldn't help grinning too.

"So what now?" she asked. "You'll be married in a month?"

Letitia nodded. "That's why we're here, actually: Mama and

I are leaving for town in a day or two, as soon as everything is packed up. I'll need to order wedding clothes and heaven knows what else, and Mama insists that only London shops are good enough for a future duchess."

Arielle's heart sank. "You're leaving so soon? I had hoped you'd stay until closer to the wedding."

"So had I. I tried to convince Mama that the modistes here are just as good—they cater to so many court ladies when they come for the season, after all—but she wouldn't hear of it. I was entirely overruled. And, you know, Papa's still in town, and he'll want to see me at least a little before I'm married off." Letitia squeezed Arielle's hand. "I will miss you, Ari, and I wish you were coming with us."

Arielle smiled sadly. "I'll miss you too. But Aunt Prissy's home is here, and she won't leave off sea-bathing until it gets too cold. You'll write to me, though, won't you?"

"Constantly," Letitia declared. "You'll hear immediately about everything I do. And you'll write back?"

"I will, but I won't have anything near as interesting to share. Without you, I won't be dragged away from my books to go on expeditions and such."

Letitia laughed. "You'll be safer, though—I'll never forget that it was my fault you were on that boat."

"But it wasn't your fault I was leaning so far over the edge. That was entirely mine."

"Oh, what a dreadful day that was!"

Arielle nodded, but she didn't entirely agree. Parts of it were awful, but the parts with Lord Patrick were not at all.

The two fell silent for a minute, then Letitia murmured, "I hope I'll hear of your own betrothal before long."

Arielle's spine stiffened. "Whatever do you mean?"

Letitia blinked at her. "Only that someone is mad about you, and I hope he hurries up and declares himself."

Arielle narrowed her eyes at her friend. "Whom do you mean?" She suspected she knew; everyone was suggesting the same person.

Letitia quickly feigned ignorance. "No one, Ari. I'm sorry—it was only speculation. I shouldn't have said anything."

"No, Letitia, you can't say something outrageous and then pretend you didn't. That's not fair. Tell me." But no amount of cajoling would bring her friend to confess the name of Arielle's admirer, and Mrs. Goulding soon rose and took leave.

Letitia gave Arielle's hands a final squeeze. "Write me. I want to hear everything, however mundane." And she left Arielle with a kiss on the cheek.

Arielle was too restless to settle with a book after that. She knew Letitia had meant Lord Patrick. The thought filled her with hope: if everyone else could see that he loved her, then Arielle must not be mistaken. If only he would call today! She finally gave up on reading and went to the kitchen to see what Mrs. Little would teach her. A walk was what she needed, but she could lose herself in flour and butter and eggs for a while.

At last, just before dinner, Lord Patrick was announced. Arielle was disappointed that he'd come too late to walk, but she was never sorry to see him. He seemed agitated, however, and his customary smile was strained. He refused the chair Olivia offered him, declaring that he could only stay a minute.

"I must beg you to allow me to postpone our walk, Miss Arielle," he said. "I must accompany my mother to town. We leave early tomorrow morning."

Aunt Prissy exclaimed at the suddenness of the departure. Arielle simply stared, dumbstruck.

## CHAPTER 19

"My brother will be leaving tomorrow as well. It seems that all the wedding preparations are to happen in London."

"But why must *you* go?" Arielle blurted. "The wedding's not for another month."

"I handle all legal matters for the Marsham family," Lord Patrick explained. "I must draw up the settlement papers between my brother and the Gouldings."

"But…"

"I did warn you that most of us would leave Brighton," he said gently.

Arielle's shoulders slumped. "I didn't realize you meant everyone would go all at once." She sounded like a petulant child, and she knew it. But it had been hard enough to hear that Letitia was leaving. Losing Lord Patrick too, and so immediately, was a blow.

"I was only told this morning that I would be required to join them."

Aunt Prissy assured him that, while he would be missed in Brighton, they understood that his duty lay with his family. He bowed, wishing them all a pleasant autumn, but his smile was gone. He took his leave and strode through the door. Olivia, standing near Arielle, placed a hand on her lower back and gave her a gentle push after him. Arielle obeyed, following Lord Patrick into the hall.

"Will you—" She hesitated, nervous. He paused by the street door and turned. "Will you come back to Brighton after the wedding, or do you intend to go straight on to Kent?"

He took a step nearer. "Do you want me to come back to Brighton?" His gray eyes searched her face. She nodded. His mouth softened. "Then that's what I'll do."

"Promise?" she whispered.

He crossed to her. "I promise." He kissed her forehead then left the house.

Arielle stood frozen in place, her skin burning where his warm lips had brushed against her. Olivia came up beside her and put an arm around her waist.

"What was he saying about a walk, Ari?"

"He'd said he'd call to walk out with me this week," she said faintly. Her regret at the loss of the walk and the chance to explain was nothing to her dismay that he was leaving altogether, and for at least a month.

"He'll be back, dear, I've no doubt." Olivia gave Arielle's waist a squeeze, then let her go. "When you're ready, come to dinner."

Arielle nodded. She slipped up the stairs to her room, closing the door behind her and leaning against it. She closed her eyes, remembering the warmth of his kiss on her forehead and his soft, "I promise." Livvie was right: he would be back. Arielle simply had to wait and trust that nothing would keep him, that he'd come back in plenty of time before her year and a day were up.

# Chapter 20

The departure of the Duke of Marsham was the first of a wave of seasonal visitors leaving Brighton. Arielle had to admit that Lord Patrick had been right when he'd guessed that she'd like the town better without all the extra people. She could shop without colliding with anyone, and the books she wanted were almost always on the shelf at the library. There were fewer morning visits, so Arielle spent more time with Olivia and Aunt Prissy, catching up on the lessons they'd started during the last rainy days. Her seams were straighter when she sewed now, thanks to all the extra practice.

But everything felt bland to Arielle. She hadn't realized until they were gone just how much Letitia had livened her days or how much she liked knowing that Lord Patrick was nearby. If she read something amusing, she wondered if he'd read the book and was disappointed he wasn't around to discuss it.

The balls at the Old Ship were the worst of it, with so many fewer people. Less crowding should have made them more pleasant, but Arielle found all her partners tedious and irritating. Lord Preston and Mr. Sharpton both did their best to be agreeable, but Arielle had no patience for anything more than common civility. She sat out the waltz entirely.

Lady Priscilla expressed concern after a full week of this dullness. "I'm sorry that Brighton is not the exciting place that it used to be," she said. "It is hard when so many friends leave for the season."

Guilt smote Arielle. She didn't want Aunt Prissy to think that she didn't like living here anymore, or that she was ungrateful. "I don't need it to be exciting," she said. "Honestly, I don't miss having parties every other day, and it's nice to have space to walk on the Steine without worrying about someone stepping on one's hem."

Aunt Prissy raised her eyebrows expectantly.

"But, yes, there are friends I wish were still here."

Aunt Prissy smiled. "That's only natural, dear. I'm sure they miss you just as much."

Arielle doubted that Letitia had much time for missing her, what with the duke's company and the entertainments of London. She'd written once already, two full pages about shops and modistes and milliners and wedding florists. But Lord Patrick... Was it awful that she hoped that he was just as distracted and incapable of enjoying company as she was? Every ball and engagement seemed superlatively stupid without him. No one said anything intelligent—it was all noise and hot air.

She borrowed the biography of Edward the Confessor that Lord Patrick had taken from the library that day, and she tried valiantly to read it. She missed hearing him talk about history and hoped to sound a little more intelligent when they next discussed the subject. But the book was dry and tedious. She found nothing about it as interesting as she would if he'd told her the facts himself.

Arielle did her best to appear cheerful, and she succeeded

most of the time. It was easiest when she was at home; daily activities with the Farleys were always comfortable and often amusing. Arielle's first attempt at planning a family dinner and arranging things with the cook left them in fits of giggles at the table. Hessy still slept in Arielle's bed at night, and Bingley was her constant, adoring shadow. Her guardians made no further comment on her mood, but they exchanged knowing glances, and they didn't argue when Arielle suggested that perhaps they could stay home the next Thursday night instead of going dancing at the Old Ship.

They did insist, however, on taking her to the theater. Her time in town had been so occupied thus far that they hadn't gone, but *A Midsummer Night's Dream* was playing, and Olivia refused to miss it.

Arielle entered the theater arm in arm with Livvie. It was a splendid building, with crystal chandeliers and scarlet curtains. They had a private box to themselves, though several people stopped by to say hello on their way to their own seats. Arielle settled in to enjoy the show.

By intermission, she was ready to concede that the theater had been a wonderful idea. She'd been laughing all through the first act, spurred on by Aunt Prissy's chuckles and Olivia's unladylike snorts of laughter beside her. The only drawbacks to the evening so far were knowing that Letitia would have delighted in the comedy and wishing she could have shared the laughter with Lord Patrick.

The curtain fell, and everyone stood and stretched and socialized while they waited for the second act to begin. Half of Brighton seemed to be out tonight, and most of them seemed to think it their duty to greet Lady Priscilla, so the box had a steady stream of visitors.

Mr. Sharpton came by to ask how they were enjoying the show. "I could see into your box from across the way, and I don't know that I've ever seen you laugh so much," he said to Arielle. "I confess, I enjoyed watching you enjoy the play more than watching the play itself."

Arielle, confused and uncomfortable, said something benign about what an amusing play it was. "I haven't read any Shakespeare. Now I see I've been missing out. Have you read many of his plays?"

"None," he said carelessly. "Why read them when you can see them in such pleasant company?"

Arielle realized with alarm that he was attempting to flirt with her. The attempt was both clumsy and unwelcome, and it was with great distress that she heard Aunt Prissy invite Mr. Sharpton to remain in their box for the second act when the lights went down. She gave Aunt Prissy a pointed look, but her guardian ignored it. Arielle sat back down in her seat and prepared to ignore their new companion for the rest of the evening.

It wasn't so easy. He leaned over to murmur comments on the actors and the setting whenever there was a brief lull between scenes. Arielle answered with the barest modicum of civility, unwilling to be rude in front of Aunt Prissy and Olivia, but wishing she could give him the cut direct. She kept her eyes on the stage, hoping that he would take the hint, but she felt his gaze on her. The attention distracted her, so that she couldn't enjoy the performance as she had in the first act. She smiled, but she didn't laugh.

It was a relief when the lights came up again after the curtain call. Arielle wanted nothing more than to get away from Mr. Sharpton. But there were yet more friends to speak to, and

## CHAPTER 20

before they could leave the theater, they were met by Mrs. Ingersoll, Miss Rowles, and Miss Crewe.

Arielle had always thought the young ladies terribly silly, but she let them draw her aside, away from Sharpton. Unsurprisingly, they had nothing but gossip to discuss. After a few opening tidbits, Miss Crewe brought up their friends in London.

"Have you had a letter from Miss Goulding, Miss Arielle?"

"Just on Tuesday," Arielle said. "She's enjoying town, though it's rather empty at this time of year, and has been spending most of her time shopping and getting to know His Grace's family."

"Speaking of His Grace's family," put in Miss Rowles with a glint in her eye, "did she mention anything about his younger brother?"

Arielle's stomach fluttered. "Lord Patrick? No, not a word. Why?"

The two girls exchanged a look. "Nancy had a letter from a friend in town just today," Miss Rowles said, gesturing at her older sister. The widow was talking with Olivia and Mr. Sharpton and paid them no notice. "The rumor among the *ton* is that Lord Patrick Alexander will soon be paying his addresses to a young lady, one of his brother's former favorites, no less."

Arielle blinked stupidly, her brain and heart both seeming to grind to a halt. Her first reaction was to disregard the rumor as false, but she had no grounds on which to base either belief or denial. "Do you know who she is?"

Miss Rowles shook her head. "But she's rumored to have an impressive dowry, and her uncle's in the House of Lords."

"The Duke of Marsham has any number of former favorites who could fit that description," Miss Crewe said dismissively.

"None of them can hold a candle to Letitia Goulding, of course, but any one would be a good catch for a third son."

"And it's not a stretch of the imagination to believe that one of them might be willing to substitute the younger brother for the elder," Miss Rowles giggled. "He hasn't got a title, and he isn't as jolly, but he's still quite handsome."

Arielle was grateful to Aunt Prissy for calling her to go home then. She didn't know what she would have said next, or if she would have simply stood in statuesque shock until dawn. Her mind felt disconnected from her body as she walked to the hired carriage. She didn't think the girls had shared the news with her vindictively; they were deplorably empty-headed, but not malicious. They couldn't have known how Arielle felt about Lord Patrick or how much such a rumor would wound her.

Arielle didn't sleep that night. She lay awake, her heart pulled in every direction. On the one hand, Lord Patrick had promised to return. On the other, Miss Rowles made a good point that it wasn't a stretch to imagine a lady willing to accept Lord Patrick in place of Marsham. He was young, handsome, kind, and from a very good family. And he would have every reason to court a well-bred lady with a dowry and a titled family. If it was an established fact that Marsham couldn't have married a nobody like Arielle, why wouldn't his brother be held to the same standards?

By morning, Arielle's mood was grayer than ever. She'd been planning to write to Letitia after going to the theater, so she did, and she gave her all the details about the performance and Mr. Sharpton's attentions, only neglecting to mention her conversation after the show. She wanted to ask Letitia if the rumor was true, but she didn't dare. A definite confirmation

## CHAPTER 20

would be unbearable.

Arielle sealed the letter but remained at her desk, thinking. What she'd felt for Marsham was a passing fancy, and her heart had been relatively untouched when he'd chosen Letitia instead. If Lord Patrick made the same choice, however… She would not emerge unscathed. She would shatter. She loved him, so deeply that there didn't seem to be a part of her that wouldn't break if he chose another. Love had crept up on her, growing without her even knowing it had begun.

She knew whom she had to marry to fulfill the magic. But she also knew that, whatever the mysterious consequences for failure, living the rest of her life without Lord Patrick would be infinitely worse.

Two days later, Olivia cornered Arielle after breakfast. "Something's wrong, and you're going to tell me what it is. Was it the theater? Did Mr. Sharpton say something?" She took Arielle by the elbow and led her to the couch in the drawing room.

Arielle shook her head. She didn't want to talk about any of it, but she most certainly didn't want to discuss Mr. Sharpton.

"I'm worried about you, Ari. You haven't been yourself since everyone left, but now…" She frowned. "You've lost your sparkle."

Bingley rested her head on Arielle's lap with a sigh, as if to add her agreement to Olivia's concern. Arielle couldn't bear to let her friends worry. Livvie's sympathy might be even worse, but there was no help for it. Arielle told Olivia what Miss Rowles and Miss Crewe had told her.

"Gammon," Olivia said bluntly. "There's not a bit of truth to it. You haven't gotten yourself all twisted up over such a nonsense rumor, have you?"

Arielle bowed her head.

Olivia tutted. "Really, Ari, we've said it enough times—the man has been in love with you for ages."

"But what if he's forgotten me since he's been gone? What if his family convinces him… I can't compete with another Incomparable like Letitia."

"Oh, stuff, he couldn't forget you if he tried, and his family likes you. You have nothing to worry about. He'll be back in Brighton after the wedding, I'm sure of it."

Arielle wished she was sure of it too. But she couldn't shake the knowledge that she lacked so many of the things a gentleman looked for in a wife. Did he love her enough to counterbalance that?

"Livvie," she said slowly, giving voice to a question she'd wondered for a while, "if you're such a romantic, why have you never married?"

Olivia smiled wistfully. "I was engaged once, a long time ago. I was about your age, maybe a little older. He was a clergyman, the second son of an earl, and he had a smile that could light up the world. He loved people and worked each day to make someone's life a little brighter."

"What happened?"

"Scarlet fever," Olivia said simply. "Two months before we were to wed, he sickened and died. I was devastated, of course, and when Aunt Prissy invited me to live as her companion, I came here. My parents thought the sea-bathing would do me good, and in a resort town like Brighton, I was sure to meet someone else."

"You didn't?"

"No one could measure up to Paul."

"Oh."

## CHAPTER 20

Olivia rested her hand on Arielle's. "Don't be sad for me, dear. I've loved my life here with Aunt Prissy, and I wouldn't trade it. And now we have you." She smiled and kissed the side of Arielle's head.

"Was Aunt Prissy ever in love?"

Olivia laughed. "No. She's been an independent soul for her whole life. I can't imagine a man who could keep up with her."

# Chapter 21

Patrick wasn't aware of being unusually irritable, so he was surprised when Frederick took him aside. Frederick was eight-and-twenty and as tall as Michael, but without the duke's athletic build. A perpetual worry line creased between his brown eyes.

"Michael told me about your girl," Frederick said, gesturing to one of the leather chairs before the fire in his study and sitting in the other.

Patrick sank into the offered chair, frowning at the fire. In the last two weeks, he'd received advice from both Michael and their mother as to what to do about Ari, and he wasn't eager to have Frederick's opinion too.

"Care to tell me about her—Miss Farley, is it?"

Patrick cringed, but Frederick must not have been told about Ari's spinster guardians. "Miss Arielle Farley, and not particularly." He shot a look at his brother. "What did Michael say?"

"That you've been in love with her for the past two months, and you're an idiot to be waiting so long to offer." Frederick waited for a response, but Patrick only scowled. "Why haven't you offered yet? I know you too well—you're not an idiot or a coward. You have a reason for waiting this long." Frederick steepled his fingers and waited again.

Patrick sighed. Frederick *did* know him, better than anyone, being only eighteen months his elder. But it was painful to speak the truth aloud, even to him. "She fancied Michael first," he muttered. "You know how he is, he charms everyone, and even I couldn't tell if he preferred her or Miss Goulding. And when he made his preference known…" Patrick shrugged. "I had to give her time to get over him."

"You didn't want to catch her on the rebound? Most men would."

Patrick shook his head. "Not from Michael. I… I want her to love me for me, not because I'm his brother. I don't want to be 'close enough' or second best. I'd rather not have her at all than have her like that."

Frederick nodded thoughtfully. Patrick knew that if anyone could understand how he felt about being in Michael's shadow, it was their middle brother. "And is she over him?"

"I think so?" Patrick shrugged. "It's been so hard to tell."

He'd been thinking of little but Arielle over the past few weeks, and he still couldn't make sense of the signals she'd been sending. There was the day he'd rescued her from drowning, when he'd been almost sure she'd welcome a kiss, and then the day after, when she hadn't met his eyes at all. And the night of the betrothal announcement, when she'd run from the ball—he couldn't make heads or tails of her behavior.

The one bright spot that he clung to was how she'd responded to his impending departure. She'd been disappointed, visibly so, and she'd even made him promise to return to Brighton. It had been impetuous to kiss her, but he hadn't been able to stop himself. She hadn't seemed to mind, though, and it had given him hope, if not confidence.

"Why haven't you gone back to Brighton? Now that the documents are all signed, you won't be needed again until the wedding itself."

Patrick slumped back in his chair. He'd debated going back. Daily. He gave his brother the same argument he'd used on himself. "What am I supposed to do, claim her heart and then disappear again? That's no way to court a woman." If he ever gained Ari's love, he wouldn't be able to tear himself away. Although he couldn't deny that being allowed to write to her would have made this separation more bearable. All he had were the tidbits Miss Goulding shared from her own correspondence.

"So you're waiting until after the wedding."

Patrick nodded.

Frederick sighed. "In that case, I'm going to have to ask you to do your best to keep your distance from Mary."

Patrick frowned in confusion. What did his relationship with Arielle have to do with Frederick's expectant wife?

"In her current condition, you know, her emotions are... unpredictable." The crease between Frederick's brows deepened, and he avoided looking at Patrick. "And you, well, you're not yourself at the moment. I've never seen you less amiable." He glanced at Patrick and away again. "You know I love you, but if you're not going to settle things with Miss Farley for another couple of weeks, I can't let your bad mood exacerbate my wife's. It's not good for the baby or for anyone else."

Patrick continued to think about this conversation for the rest of the day. It wasn't hard to avoid Mary during the day, but sitting down to dinner was inevitable, unless he found an engagement elsewhere. Which was why he knocked on Michael's door late in the afternoon. The duke's Mayfair

## CHAPTER 21

residence was easily twice the size of Frederick's home, but it was just as familiar to Patrick, having lived in the house during visits to town when their father was alive.

"What brings you here?" Michael asked when Patrick was shown into the parlor. "I thought you'd had enough of me in Brighton."

So had Patrick. But brothers were brothers. "Am I more irritable than normal?" he asked bluntly.

Michael laughed. "Why are you asking? Are you losing patience with Mary's moods?"

Patrick glared his boots. "No. Frederick said my mood is making hers worse."

Michael laughed harder, then poured them each a glass of brandy and handed one to Patrick. "And he told you to come bother me?"

"Not necessarily. Only to make myself scarce."

Michael grinned and sipped his drink. "And this wasn't enough of a clue for you, so you had to come ask me as well?"

Patrick glowered at him.

"See? Right there. I might as well be facing down a bear. Frederick's right, little brother—you're an irritable nightmare."

"Great. Thanks." Patrick set his undrunk glass on a table and turned to leave.

"Don't be a fool," Michael said. "You know what the solution is."

"I'm not going back to Brighton until after the wedding."

"But you're going back?"

Patrick nodded.

"And you'll finally ask her?"

Another nod.

"Then I suppose I can tolerate you for a few hours. Have

dinner here tonight. Letitia and her parents are supposed to be dining with us, and Letitia's due for another letter."

Patrick had been about to decline the invitation—if he really was a bear, he didn't need to spend the evening with the Gouldings and his mother—but Michael had hit on the one thing that would make him stay.

He was on his best behavior through dinner. Anyone who knew him well could have seen that he was not as cheerful as usual, but at least he didn't snap at anyone, and he kept his scowling to a minimum. They joined the ladies in the drawing room not long after they'd retired there after dinner; Patrick was impatient to hear of any letter, and for once, Michael decided not to trifle with him.

Mother and Mrs. Goulding were talking of Mrs. Goulding's plan to redecorate her drawing room and were deep in discussion about drapes and wallpapers. Mr. Goulding joined them. Michael easily drew Letitia aside.

"My love, have you had any letters from Brighton lately?"

Letitia flashed a bright smile at Patrick. "I had one just this morning."

"Is there any news you can share? Has Sharpton offered yet?"

Patrick glared at Michael, who grinned back.

"Not yet," Letitia said. "Though he was beyond attentive at the theater. He joined them at intermission and stayed through the second act, blatantly flirting."

Patrick's stomach had dropped to the floor, and he was losing the battle for composure. He had to clasp his hands behind his back to hide his clenched fists.

Letitia raised her delicately arched eyebrows. "Are you jealous, Patrick? You needn't be. She doesn't like him." She smiled with feigned innocence. "Have I told you how much I'd love to have Ari for a sister?"

Heat was rising in Patrick's neck, and his cravat felt uncomfortably tight. "Would she like it as well?" he asked. The only way for the girls to be sisters was for Ari to marry Patrick.

"Oh, more than anything." The arch look she gave said she understood his meaning. "She's liked you forever."

"But liking someone and wanting to marry them are very different things."

"Michael, your brother is being intentionally dense."

"That's not new," Michael agreed amiably. "He's been nonsensical about Arielle Farley from the moment he set eyes on her."

Letitia considered Patrick. "*I* thought you ought to have asked her right after the boating incident. I was nearly in hysterics, and I *still* noticed how you two were looking at each other."

The flush was creeping up Patrick's face now. He almost wished he'd gone to the club to eat alone. Hearing of Ari wasn't worth facing the inquisition. Except that it was. He was so desperate for news of her.

"I'm intending to write her back tomorrow," Letitia added. "Is there any message you'd like to relay?"

Nothing that Patrick really wanted to say could be relayed through his soon-to-be sister-in-law. But he wasn't willing to pass up this opportunity, either. He couldn't tell her how much he missed her or how he couldn't get her out of his head. He couldn't ask permission to write to her himself. Patrick turned away from the others, thinking back over conversations he'd had with Ari, trying to find a way to hint at his hopes without being indiscreet. His gaze fell on a small stack of books on an end table.

"Would you tell her that there is truth in *Pride and Prejudice*, both in the passage she read aloud and in the very first sentence?"

Letitia surveyed him quizzically, but nodded. "Her favorite book. You really are perfect for each other," she said softly.

\*\*\*

*It is a truth universally acknowledged, that a single man in possession of a good fortune, must be in want of a wife.*

Why had Lord Patrick asked Letitia to tell her that? And why send her a message now, when he hadn't in either of Letitia's earlier letters?

Of course Arielle remembered asking him the question as they'd walked from the library. It was one of her favorite memories, just the two of them, relaxed and happy. But why had he drawn her attention back to it? Was he telling her that he hoped she'd be his wife? Or was he telling her that he was marrying someone else and wouldn't be coming back to Brighton after all?

Arielle thought of him in a church in London, marrying a perfect bride, who, in Arielle's imagination, looked a lot like Letitia, with the golden curls and elegant posture. He'd take that new wife directly home to his charming country house in Kent. Arielle felt ill. She'd been fascinated by Lord Patrick's house since hearing him tell of it—it seemed to her like a combination of Longbourn and Barton Cottage, the homes of Jane Austen's heroines—and she'd clung to a half-formed wish of seeing it. Now, with the sickening vision of another woman making herself at home there, Arielle understood why it held such sway in her mind: it was *his* house, and she wanted to be there with *him*.

Arielle took the letter with her to the beach, crumpled

now after so many readings. She'd read the two sentences pertaining to Lord Patrick a dozen times, only to put the missive down and pick it back up a moment later. Maybe it would all be clearer with the breeze in her face and the surf in her ears.

Of course, the beach itself reminded her of him. She'd stood close to him for dizzy, beautiful moments, with his focus all on her.

What was he trying to tell her?

There couldn't be any truth in the Netherfield scene she'd read at the Gouldings' dinner party, could there? It was all Lizzy and Darcy bantering. Was he comparing himself to Darcy? And if that was the case, was she Lizzy? Did he secretly love her, despite all objections?

It was too much to hope. Arielle wished she could believe it. She thought—sometimes—that he cared for her. He noticed how she felt; he was aware of what she needed. But that was just who he was, thoughtful and kind and good. Were his feelings stronger than that? Were they strong enough to stand up against the social pressure that told him to choose someone with all the money and connections that she lacked?

Arielle stared out at the waves. The wind whipped locks of hair from the pins that held them, but she did nothing to push them away from her face. White foam-topped breakers rolled in, reminding Arielle of the night she'd run to the sea for answers. The unknown had consumed her then; the magic that hid her missing past had loomed so large it obscured everything else. But now... what did it matter? The prospect of losing Patrick forever put all her other troubles into a new perspective. Her past was irrelevant. Her present included a family who loved her, who had welcomed her in with open arms, and friends she cared about deeply. And her future... her future was a confusing tangle. She hoped—dreamed, longed—for the possible future that included Patrick. If not, her year and a day would end and... whatever happened next would happen. Her broken heart would eventually mend, but she'd never fall in love again.

She sighed. Her origins would remain a secret. But that, for once, felt acceptable. She'd come from the sea, and that was enough. The sea was vast enough to be her whole past. What mattered now was moving forward.

Arielle hoped and prayed with every ounce of her being that Patrick would come again, unmarried, to move forward with her.

# Chapter 22

Arielle was sitting in her favorite chair by the window in the parlor the day after the wedding. Hessy was curled on her lap, and Bingley warmed her feet. She'd been reading Miss Austen's *Emma*, which she ought to have found amusing, but today it felt abysmally stupid. Emma's penchant for playing matchmaker didn't suit Arielle's mood at all. By now the Duke and Duchess of Marsham would be on their way to Italy for their honeymoon. Letitia had written in her last letter about their plans and what she hoped to see.

By now, the family who had come to town for the wedding would be going their separate ways.

Arielle sighed and tried to be interested in Emma's foolish machinations. A minute later, Olivia's voice in the hall distracted her. Livvie sounded like she was talking to a guest, not Aunt Prissy or one of the household servants, but a guest ought to have been brought to the drawing room, not the family's private parlor. The knob turned, and Olivia pushed open the door and came in, talking over her shoulder to their visitor.

"Ari has been so very blue since you all left last month. I do hope you can cheer her up. I'll go call for tea."

And then Olivia was gone, closing the door behind her.

Arielle, oblivious to the speech and subsequent disappearance of her chaperone, got to her feet, tumbling both book and cat from her lap and dislodging Bingley. Lord Patrick stood before her, as handsome and well turned out as ever. His gray eyes held hers with a promise of never letting go.

"You came back," she said.

"I promised I would." His voice, rich and warm, washed over her like a cup of chocolate on a chill day.

"You did," she admitted, "but there was a rumor that you had found a reason to stay away."

"What reason?" He looked surprised and confused, and her heart leapt.

"They said you'd marry one of the Incomparables who hadn't managed to snare your brother."

He huffed a humorless laugh. "Nothing could be farther from the truth." They'd both been moving slowly toward the center of the room, and now they stood face to face, only a foot of space between them. "Is your heart still broken over Michael's choice?"

Arielle blinked at him. "It—it never was."

Patrick rubbed a hand over his face. "Don't pretend you never felt anything for him. I saw the two of you together. And when he announced his engagement…" He shook his head.

"It's more complicated than that," Arielle said gently, relieved to finally have the chance to explain. "I… somehow, I remembered your brother. I don't remember anything else, but I recognized *him*. And I remembered loving him." She saw pain flinch through his eyes. "Yes, Patrick, I was infatuated for a while. But even after it faded, I hoped that somehow I'd remember more, that he'd be the key to unlocking my past. And when their betrothal was announced, it was like… it was like I'd never known him. The change was so sudden and unexpected. It was as if that hint of memory had never even existed. I wasn't hurt that he was marrying Letitia—I'm thrilled for them both. But that last, fragile, tenuous link to my past was just... gone." Patrick reached for her hands. His were warm and strong and reassuring. "I tried to tell you that night, but I was too confused and upset to be coherent." She gave him a weak smile. "That's why I asked you to go for a walk with me—so I could explain."

"Oh, *Ari*."

"It's all right, though." His concern and sympathy warmed her, but she didn't want him to be sad for her. "I understand better now. My past isn't as important as my present. I have a good life here. And... I hoped... maybe a future... with you?"

Her voice came out softer and softer until she whispered the last words.

"With me?" he breathed.

Arielle nodded.

"Are you sure you don't see me as a mediocre substitute for Michael?"

Arielle gaped at him. "Are you serious? Patrick, I don't want your brother. And you're anything but mediocre. You're kind and thoughtful and heroic, and you love books, and you make me like history—which, believe me, I can't wrap my head around without you—and your smile is my favorite in the whole world." She pulled one hand from his and lightly ran her fingers over his cheek, where that beloved smile was slowly stretching wider. "You are *wonderful*."

Patrick leaned in then and kissed her. Arielle's knees went weak, and he let go of her other hand to wrap his arms around her waist, holding her close, supporting her, loving her. When he pulled back, it was only far enough to look her in the eye.

"I've loved you from the moment you arrived accidentally on my doorstep."

Arielle smiled. "I'm sorry it took me so long to figure out how much I love you too."

"You're worth waiting for," he said against her lips before claiming them again.

Arielle lost track of time, but it seemed much too soon when Patrick stopped kissing her. "Marry me?" he asked, pressing a kiss to her temple.

"Yes, love." Arielle attempted to straighten the cravat she'd wrinkled by throwing her arms around his neck. "But you knew that answer."

"For once, I had no doubts." He grinned. "We should probably seek out your guardian so I can ask permission."

"You mean you don't want to wait for Livvie to find us here when she finally returns with tea?" Arielle laughed. "I think refreshments were all a ruse. Her chaperoning skills are debatable."

Patrick laughed too. "Miss Farley is unconventional, I daresay," he agreed, "but I'm glad of it."

"You'll have to start calling her Livvie, you know. You're about to be family, and she won't let you stand on ceremony. Neither will Aunt Prissy."

He chuckled. "I've known Lady Priscilla since I was a child, so I don't know how easy it will be to call her that, but I'll do anything to be a family with you, Ari."

He planted one more kiss on her lips, then stepped back and took her hand. Together, they left the parlor in search of her family.

## CHAPTER 22

✳✳✳

Aunt Prissy delightedly gave her heartfelt consent. "I'm glad you came back when you did, Lord Patrick. I was beginning to worry we'd never see an Ari smile again."

Her face crinkled as she beamed at Arielle, who hadn't stopped smiling since Patrick's arrival.

"That would be devastating," Patrick agreed, casting an adoring look at Arielle.

"She moped for weeks," Olivia said.

"I wasn't particularly agreeable myself." Patrick smiled ruefully. "One of my brothers called me a bear, and the other politely requested that I stay away from his wife, because *my* irritability was increasing *hers*."

"How is Mary?" Olivia asked.

"Quite well," Patrick said. To Arielle, he added, "Frederick's wife Mary is only a little older than you, and I think you'll like her. She's a sweet girl, when I'm not making her mood swings worse."

"I'll be delighted to meet her." Arielle grinned. "To think I had no family at all so few weeks ago, and now, not only do I have a family, but I'll soon have brothers and sisters."

"Not too soon, I hope." Aunt Prissy tilted her head to study the newly betrothed pair, her expression serious but with a twinkle in her eye. "I won't insist on a long engagement, but don't be thinking of special licenses. You two ought to have a proper courtship first. And I intend to enjoy my last few weeks with Ari here."

Arielle exchanged glances with Patrick. She knew she wasn't alone in wanting to be married as soon as possible, and not only because she had a year and a day to do it, but Lady

Priscilla made a good point. She and Patrick hadn't reached an understanding until just this afternoon, and they hadn't even been in the same town for the last month. There were walks to take and questions to ask and secrets to share. But all of that would be wonderful, because Patrick was back in Brighton, and she knew without asking that he'd be spending as much of every day with her as he could.

"No special license," Patrick agreed, a wry smile hiding any disappointment. "We'll wait for the banns. I'll send the announcement to the Gazette tomorrow."

Dinner was announced, and the three ladies unanimously pressed Patrick—who needed no encouragement—to stay and dine with them. He didn't stay long after dinner that evening; he'd promised his family the earliest news of his engagement, so he had letters to write to post tomorrow.

"I'll see you in the morning," he murmured to Arielle, pausing at the front door and kissing her temple.

Arielle was too excited to see him the next day—and the next, and the next—to resent his leaving now. She returned to the sitting room and picked up the collection of Wordsworth from the table and began to read aloud.

\*\*\*

Patrick was too impatient to wait for regular calling hours the next morning. He arrived when the Farleys were sitting down to breakfast. Miss Farley—Livvie—teased him about it as she invited him to sit and eat. He sat, but he'd eaten at home. All he wanted was to be near Arielle, and from the brilliant smiles she sent his way, she was glad he'd come.

"It's a beautiful day," he said. "A bit cool, but perfect for a

## CHAPTER 22

walk. I believe I had to postpone the walk I promised you last month, Ari. Will you take it with me today?"

"That's exactly what I was going to ask you." She grinned. "I'd love to."

Patrick had a hard time sitting still as he waited for them to finish breakfast. He felt like a schoolboy waiting for a promised treat. In actual time, it didn't take Arielle long to eat and change her dress, but it felt like hours before her gloved hand was tucked into his elbow as they descended the front steps to the street. Bingley trotted at Arielle's heels, and the Farleys' abigail followed at a discreet distance.

"Where shall we walk, my love?"

"Anywhere," Arielle said with a happy shrug. "You were absolutely right when you said I'd like Brighton better after everyone had left. I didn't when *you* were gone, but I do now."

"Has everyone left?" Patrick asked. "I thought Sharpton and some of the others were still here. Didn't you see him at the theater?"

"Oh, no, did Letitia tell you about that letter?" Arielle looked aghast.

Patrick chuckled. "She did. I admit to being rather jealous when she told me he was shamelessly flirting with you, but Letitia assured me that I had nothing to worry about."

"She was quite right," Arielle said firmly. "I'd enjoyed the first half of the play immensely, but after intermission..." She made a face. "It quite put me off theater altogether."

"I hope not forever. I should like to take you sometimes."

Arielle considered him with a sparkle in her aquamarine eyes. "Shall you flirt with me shamelessly?"

The corner of Patrick's mouth kicked up. "Probably."

Arielle giggled.

They strolled along Marine Parade, and as they approached the Steine, they saw two elegant figures, arm in arm, approaching from the other direction. Miss Rowles and Miss Crewe saw them and immediately put their heads together.

"How soon do we want our engagement to be known around Brighton?" Arielle asked him, her eyes on the young ladies.

"Rumors are about to start flying, are they not?" he asked. "We might as well give them the truth to spread around."

The two young ladies hailed them now, and the four of them stopped to chat. Patrick was conscious of being the subject of curious, eager looks that confused him at first until Arielle spoke.

"I hope, Miss Rowles, that your sister's correspondent in town won't be terribly disappointed," she said with a sympathetic look. "In fact, I hope she'll be delighted to be the first to correct the false rumor that she'd heard."

"It was false, then?" Miss Rowles said avidly, with another glance at Patrick.

"Quite," Arielle said. "I accepted Lord Patrick's proposal just yesterday."

Delighted squeals burst from the two young ladies, causing Bingley to bark as well, and Arielle grinned. Congratulations followed, and the girls kissed Arielle's cheeks as though they'd been bosom friends for life. After another moment, the group separated, with Arielle trying to stifle her laugher.

"There," she said, when they were out of earshot. "What would you wager that news of our engagement will spread through most of England before the Gazette prints a word?"

Patrick laughed. "I'm glad that I've already posted the letter to Mother, then." He looked down at Arielle, who had conveniently neglected to wear her bonnet today. Her rosy hair shone in the morning sun. "I take it they were the source of the rumor you heard?"

Arielle nodded. "A friend of Mrs. Ingersoll's mentioned it."

"You didn't truly believe it, did you?"

Arielle didn't respond. She made a point of examining the books in the library window as they passed.

"Ari, love, why would you believe something like that? Had I not made it clear enough that I worship the ground you walk on?"

She looked up at him then, a playfully stern expression compressing her mouth. "Don't tease."

"Very well, I won't," Patrick said earnestly. "But tell me why you let such a story bother you."

Arielle sighed. "You would have been well within your rights to seek a woman worthy of you."

This stopped Patrick in his tracks. He turned to look at her. "What on earth do you mean?"

The playfulness had gone from Ari's face. "I'm nobody, Patrick. You know this. I have nothing to offer—no fortune, no connection, no bloodline, no skills of any kind. By all standards, you ought to look elsewhere."

"I don't need those things," he said, shaking his head, baffled. "I'm a third son with no title to hand down, and I have fortune enough myself that I can give you a comfortable home without needing more."

Arielle searched his face. "You're promising me the world," she said softly, "but what do you get out of it?"

Patrick gaped at her, incredulous. "I get *you*. You're all I want, Ari. How can I make myself clearer? I *love* you. I love talking with you and walking with you close beside me. I love how your eyes light up when you're curious about something new. I love that you abhor crowds as much as I do. I love dancing with you. I love listening to you read. I love those almost invisible freckles on your nose." He watched her cheeks get pinker and pinker as he spoke, and he darted in to brush the lightest kiss over those freckles. "I absolutely *adore* your laugh," he said, thinking of the first time he'd heard it through the window. "I've been incomplete all my life, and suddenly, when I'm with you, I feel whole. Do you see now why the very idea of me marrying anyone else is preposterous?"

Arielle's mouth had fallen open, and she was practically glowing with joy and embarrassment. "Well, I suppose…" She leaned her head against his shoulder. Patrick pressed a kiss to her silky hair.

The sound of a throat clearing behind them caused Arielle to raise her head. She glanced over her shoulder at the abigail, blushed brighter, and tugged on Patrick's arm to get him walking again. Bingley had been sniffing the steps of the library while they'd been standing there, but now she took her place by Arielle's side.

They left Marine Parade and meandered along the beach. Though the sky was partly overcast, the pebbles gleamed wetly, polished by the receding tide.

Patrick noticed again how Arielle seemed to relax even more as soon as they were near the water. Bingley took off running the length of the beach, and Arielle laughed as she watched the dog. Her laughter subsided as she turned to look out at the waves. Patrick stopped beside her, resting one hand on the small of her back, reassuring himself that she was here with him. Twice, he'd thought he was going to lose her to those waves. But standing here together, he let the rhythm of the surf relax him too.

## CHAPTER 22

"Will you teach me to swim?"

Patrick stiffened. The non sequitur was surprising, but far less than the request itself. "Even after..." He didn't want to bring up the most traumatic day in their history together. If he could avoid thinking of that panic-stricken day for the rest of his life, he'd be happy.

"Those first few seconds under the water—before I realized I couldn't get back up to breathe—were... something." She shook her head. "It just felt right. I want to be able to experience that again."

Patrick studied her face as she continued to gaze out at the water. She had a connection to the sea, subtler than her uncanny way with animals but just as real. He'd seen glimpses of it occasionally, but until now he'd been able to ignore it or pretend it was nothing. He remembered how worried he'd been the night he'd found her knee deep in the surf, and he realized that his deeper, underlying fear had been that the sea would take her back. It had tried once already, knocking her out of the boat.

Arielle's hand held loosely to Patrick's arm, and he laid his free hand over hers. Who was one man to stand against an ocean? But he refused to lose her.

"I will teach you," he said, tugging her closer and kissing the top of her head, "if you promise never to swim away and not come back."

Ari blinked up at him, startled, then laughed. Patrick let the sound wash over him and sweep his fears away. "I promise."

They walked on again, and after a few minutes of comfortable silence, Patrick asked, "What else do you want?"

"What do you mean?"

"You want to learn to swim. What else do you want your life

to hold? An unlimited supply of books to read, obviously, but what else?" He smiled at her teasingly, but he was serious, and from the thoughtful look in her bright eyes, she knew it.

"I don't know," she said finally. "I've spent all this time trying to learn how to fit in here and puzzle out the past I've forgotten. I've only just begun to look forward. I know I want to be with you. I want to waltz with you as often as possible." Patrick had the urge to spin her in his arms right there on the beach, but instead he kept walking, letting her think. "I want to bake more, and play with my furry little loves." She bent to pet Bingley, who chose that moment to press against Arielle's legs for some attention. "I've wanted to learn magic ever since Letitia's display." She shrugged and smiled up at him. "What about you?"

Patrick had spent the better part of the last two months thinking of little else, so it was an easy answer to give. "I want to make a home with you."

"You have a home," she said, confused.

"I have a house," he corrected. "*Home* means love and family and belonging and sitting together by the fire in the evenings and waking up beside you in the mornings…"

He spoke softly so the abigail wouldn't hear, and Ari's face lit with a slow smile. "I've tried so hard not to let myself dream of that," she said. "But, oh, it hurt to think of you making such a home with someone else."

"Only you, Ari," Patrick murmured, stopping and taking her in his arms. The abigail had paused nearby, averting her eyes and pretending not to see. The rest of the beach was mostly deserted. Patrick didn't care if all of Brighton saw them. He loved Arielle Farley, and he wanted her to know it. "Always only you."

# Epilogue

*Three months later*

Arielle had been gaping out the carriage window for the past half hour, ever since London had first become visible in the distance. Now well within the city, she couldn't tear her eyes away. There were so many buildings, so many people—she felt like a naïve fool for thinking Brighton crowded last summer.

"Is it always so smoky?" she murmured, aghast at the thick gray air.

Patrick slid closer to look past her out the window. "Usually," he confirmed. "It's often foggy too." He took her hand in his, and even through their gloves she could feel the comforting warmth of his grip.

"How could anyone want to live here?" Her horror must have shown on her face because Patrick chuckled.

"I've never understood it myself. You'll have to ask Frederick."

Arielle involuntarily clutched his hand tighter. She was about to meet the rest of his family for the first time. She shouldn't be nervous—she'd heard only good things about Frederick and Mary, both from Patrick and from Letitia's letters—but her instinctive reactions wouldn't listen to logic. If they didn't like her, this would be a very awkward Christmas.

Arielle and Patrick had been married in October. She'd been

flooded with a sense of rightness as she repeated her vows. The magic was complete, whatever it was, and the memory faded as if it had never existed. But that mattered little in the face of spending the rest of her life with Patrick.

The small ceremony had been held in the Brighton church, with only Aunt Prissy, Olivia, and Patrick's mother for witnesses. Michael and Letitia had still been honeymooning on the continent, and Mary's condition wouldn't allow her to travel. But now they were all gathering in London for Christmas.

Perhaps it was the closeness and heaviness of their surroundings that made Arielle nervous. Town was a very far cry from their pastoral home in Kent. Arielle missed the fresh air and open spaces already, and they'd only been gone a day. The house had been exactly as charming as she'd hoped, and she'd settled into her life there with greater ease than she'd fitted into Brighton society. Bingley, too, seemed to enjoy the country. It was quieter and more peaceful, and while Arielle had new roles to learn as a wife and the lady of the house, there were fewer people to lay claim to her time. Though she sometimes missed the ocean and the Farleys, she enjoyed the long walks that she and Patrick—and Bingley—took daily, through the woods or the fields, or into the village to the lending library. They would return to Brighton in the spring and spend all the warmer months there. But she'd be glad to always return to the country house for at least half the year. Being away from home only made her realize how much it truly had become a *home*.

"Don't worry," Patrick said, feeling her tense grip. He covered her hand with his free hand. "They'll love you. And Michael and Letitia and Mother already do."

## EPILOGUE

Arielle nodded absently. They'd be staying with the duke and duchesses, so as not to impose on Mary. While Arielle had moments of doubt whether Patrick was thrilled about the arrangement, she herself was relieved that her first visit to town would be in company with her friend.

The carriage pulled to a stop in front of a grand, stone house on Berkeley Street. It was so large that Arielle wondered at first if there'd been some mistake—had the driver brought them to an inn instead? This was certainly no smaller than the Castle Inn in Brighton. But Patrick climbed from the carriage as soon as a footman opened the door, then handed a stunned Arielle down. She gladly took his arm for the short walk to the front door.

The butler who opened the door had sleek white hair and a face as full of wrinkles as Aunt Prissy, although his seemed to come from scowling sternly rather than laughing. But he greeted Patrick warmly and by name, and he took their coats, hats, and gloves before directing them to the family parlor. Arielle gazed about in wonder. Some of the homes she'd visited in Brighton had been fine, but this was elegance itself. Marble and gold, velvet and brocade, alabaster statues and cut glass vases of hothouse flowers.

Arielle realized after a moment that her mouth had fallen open, and that Patrick was watching her with an amused twinkle in his eye. She closed her mouth with a snap.

"It's a bit much, I think," he murmured. "Very grand, of course, but not quite comfortable."

She smiled at him. He somehow always knew exactly what to say to put her at ease. The house was indeed intimidating, and not least because this is what Patrick had grown up with, what he was used to. She'd felt alone in feeling out of place, but now she leaned her head against his shoulder for a moment, relaxing in a sense of togetherness. He kissed her head and rested his cheek against her hair.

The door opened, and they straightened, turning to Letitia, who somehow made racing into a room to tug her friend into a hug look as graceful as dancing.

"You're here! You're finally here!" Letitia gushed, squeezing Arielle.

"Thank you for letting us stay."

"Don't be silly, we only wish you were staying longer." Letitia looked over her shoulder at Marsham, who had entered behind her. He shook hands all around, seconding his wife's welcome and asking Patrick about their journey. While the brothers talked about roads, carriages, and tolls, Letitia drew Arielle down onto a sofa beside her.

"I have been dying for months to ask you about that cryptic message I relayed for Patrick," Letitia said. "Did you understand it right away? What did he mean by it?"

Arielle laughed. "I did understand it, or nearly. He was hinting that he'd loved me even when I was unaware, and that he wanted to marry me—"

"If only he'd sent that message earlier!" Letitia interrupted. "You would have been spared weeks of discomfort."

Arielle shook her head. "Or it would have made them worse. I didn't tell you about the rumor I'd heard from Miss Rowles at the theater that Patrick would be marrying a lady he knew here in town. Half of his message could have easily applied to her as well."

"Nonsense, Ari," Letitia protested. "How could he have married anyone else after he saved you from drowning like that?" Arielle opened her mouth to point out that he would have saved anyone from drowning if he could, but Letitia prevented her by saying, "Why didn't you ask me about the rumor? I could have denied it right away."

"Or you could have confirmed it. Little hope seemed better than none."

Letitia sighed. "Oh, Ari, this is my fault. I should have pestered Patrick to write to you himself. I thought of it—I could easily have tucked a letter from him into one of my own."

A lull in the brothers' conversation allowed them to hear this last comment. With a smirk at his brother, Michael said, "It wouldn't have worked. Frederick and I had been after him to go back to Brighton, and he wouldn't do that either."

"Why on earth not?" Letitia asked.

"He claimed that he wouldn't propose only to leave again." Michael's smirk grew.

"We could have written then," Arielle said softly, her eyes on Patrick. "I'm sure we would both have been less miserable."

"Perhaps." Patrick held her gaze. "But once I knew you loved me, I would not have had the strength to drive away."

Arielle bit her lip, warmth rising to her face.

"Water under the bridge, I suppose," Letitia said. "You're married, and you're here, and we're going to have a lovely time."

Letitia had thoughtfully arranged to have a small family dinner, just the two couples and the dowager duchess, to give Arielle and Patrick a quiet night to recover from their travels.

The next morning, they called in Portman Square. They were shown into the parlor, where Mary was reclining on a couch and Frederick was sitting in an armchair with a book. He put down the book and got to his feet as Patrick introduced

Arielle, coming over to shake hands. He was taller than Patrick, with a thoughtful face and dark eyes. He greeted them with a smile and introduced Arielle to Mary, who struggled to a sitting position.

"Please don't get up on my account," Arielle said, hurrying over and settling onto an ottoman near Mary's couch. "We're sisters now—no standing on ceremony." She caught Patrick's grin at the familiar words: she was a Farley through and through.

Mary sighed and settled back against the cushions. Her dark hair was pinned loosely up, and her blue eyes were bright as she looked Arielle over. They would probably have been about the same size, if Mary had not been seven months along in her pregnancy. "I've been so looking forward to meeting you," Mary said. "Poor Patrick had to put up with me when he was in town for the wedding, and I was afraid he'd keep you away rather than risking me frightening you off."

"I heard *you* had to put up with *him*," Arielle said with a smile. "And I don't think you could frighten anyone."

Mary chuckled. "You'd be surprised. Patrick and Frederick have had the worst of it, I think." She studied Arielle's face for a moment. "Tell me about yourself. I've heard bits and pieces from everyone, and I can see with my own eyes why Patrick fell so hard so quickly, but it's not the same as a good chat."

So Arielle told Mary about the Farleys taking her in and about her obsession with books. She told her about Patrick teaching them how to waltz. Mary told Arielle about her first meeting with Frederick, which had been at a private ball. He'd asked her to dance, but without paying attention to which he was asking for. When the quadrille was announced, he'd gone very pale and asked if she minded walking about with him instead, as he didn't know the steps.

"I thought it rather brave of him to own up to the fault," Mary said, sending her husband a loving look. "And he was so handsome that I didn't mind what we did, as long as I could be with him. After that, he was careful to specify which dance."

Arielle laughed, and she felt Patrick's eyes on her. She glanced over and found him smiling, and she knew he was glad she'd made a new friend in the family.

Letitia and Arielle had their own *tête-à-tête* in the sitting room the following day. Letitia had been sending Arielle simple, easy spells to try in some of her letters, and now she insisted that Ari demonstrate her progress.

"It's not great progress," Arielle said, but she spoke a spell word and lit a nearby candle, then spoke another to snuff it out. "That's about all I've managed so far."

"But you're doing really well," Letitia told her. "The first few spells are the hardest until you get the feel for it. Now that you've managed to do those, the magic will come more easily and feel more natural."

To prove her point, she taught Arielle another spell, to levitate an object and move it. She demonstrated by lifting her teacup and moving it several inches to one side, without the tea splashing at all. Arielle didn't dare try it on her teacup, so she concentrated on a biscuit from the tray. She moved it to her plate, making it almost all the way before she dropped it onto the table. Letitia clapped, and Arielle grinned. It was such a small thing, but she felt proud of the tiny accomplishment. She picked up the biscuit from where it fell and took a bite.

On Christmas, they all went to dinner at Frederick's. It was a cheerful, amiable group: the three brothers, their wives, and their mother. Arielle had wondered at first if Patrick's mother would disapprove of her, regardless of how *he* felt about her lack of connections or fortune, but she'd welcomed Arielle into the family and insisted that she call her "Mother" like the rest.

It was a cozy family party that gathered in the parlor after dinner, and gifts were exchanged. This was Arielle's first Christmas, the first she could remember, and she'd enjoyed choosing gifts with Patrick. He'd had great fun telling her about the holiday and about some of his favorite Christmas memories from childhood. Arielle blushed with delight when she received her first gift, a beginner spell book from Letitia. When she opened her gifts from Frederick and Mary and from Mother, her eyes welled up: both volumes of *Persuasion*, the latest novel from Miss Austen, who would write no more.

Her voice shook as she thanked them, touched at their understanding and thoughtfulness. Patrick put his arm around her, and she snuggled close against him. She had two families now, the Farleys and the Alexanders, and she loved them all. Filled with a sense of belonging that continued to surprise and amaze, Arielle smiled up at Patrick. He kissed her temple, and she knew: here with him, with this family—despite the dirty, cramped city just outside the doors—she was home.

Want more magic in Regency England? Read on for chapter 1 of *Her Cursed Apple*, a retelling of "Snow White."

*EPILOGUE*

# Her Cursed Apple: Chapter 1

Winston's mouth dropped open in horror. Bianca ignored him, scooting further into the hollow beneath the fallen trees that had fit them so much better when they were younger. She settled across from him, her knees in her lightweight cotton riding habit pressing against his. Her friend had shot up like a weed a few years ago, and now his tall, lanky frame was the main reason they were outgrowing their childhood hideout.

Still ignoring Winston's scowl, only somewhat hidden by the dark blond curls that tumbled over his forehead and blue eyes, she pulled a napkin of stolen honey almond biscuits from her pocket and unwrapped them, offering him one.

"Bribes won't work," he grumbled. "It's gone too far."

Bianca glared at him, daring him to say another word, to say that her clandestine pugilism lessons needed to end. He'd said it enough times over the past six years that she knew exactly what was coming.

Rather than squirming under her glare like he used to, Winston leaned forward, his frown both earnest and regretful. "This one's worse than the last," he said, his eyes perusing her face where a puffy, purplish bruise graced her cheekbone and partially obscured her right eye.

"It was an accident." Bianca shrugged. "Any fighter has to be prepared to take a few hits. I'm not hurt, nor am I frightened to be hurt in the future."

"But you're *not* a fighter," Winston protested. "You're a young lady, and if I'm to have any hope of being a man of honor, I can't raise a fist against you anymore. I—"

"Should have stopped years ago, I know," Bianca sighed. "You've told me. A hundred times."

After a brief silence, Winston said, "What tale did you spin this time?"

"No need. Papa is still in town, and the servants all generously pretend not to know what I get up to. Nurse tutted over me a bit, but she looks the other way even better than everyone else." Bianca's smile was a little crooked because of her puffy eye, but it was genuine. She loved Nurse, who had been the nearest thing she'd had to a mother for most of her life.

Relaxing slightly, she took a bite of one biscuit and offered the other to Winston again. He sighed and took it, studying it broodingly for a moment before swallowing the whole thing in two bites.

Bianca couldn't help remembering the first time they'd had this same conversation. She'd been nine; Winston had been just starting his proper lessons with his new tutor at age twelve. One of his lessons had been pugilism, and he'd promised to teach her everything he learned, but he'd accidentally given her a black eye during their first practice and refused to teach her more. She *had* needed to lie to Papa about that one. She'd claimed that her horse Diamond had spooked and run, and she'd hit her face on a branch. To her dismay, Papa had insisted a groom accompany her on her rides.

She glanced out of the tree cave toward where Harry stood with the horses. Who knew that the groom her father had assigned to her was a former bare-knuckle boxer and prizefighter? He'd agreed to give them both lessons in the interest of saving their friendship after he overheard Bianca threatening to never speak to Winston again if he went back on his promise. It had been six years, and Bianca secretly thought that they were probably both good enough to go a round with any prizefighter in England. And Harry had become more a friend and teacher than a servant by now.

"Has your father written to say when he'll arrive home?"

"Three weeks. They hoped to hold the wedding before the end of the Season and all their potential guests left town."

"Late May is cutting it close. Mother and I weren't the only ones who left at the end of April."

Bianca shrugged. "I guess that was the soonest she could be ready. My new stepmother." She said the word with trepidation, testing it, tasting it to see if it would be bitter or sweet. When she was younger, she often wished for a mother, a warm, loving figure to fill the void left by the one she could barely remember. She had wished for siblings, too—younger brothers and sisters to fill Eston Hall and provide playmates for those rainy days when she couldn't ride out to meet Winston in the woods. Now, though, she was fifteen, and she no longer needed a playmate. She would be grown and married and moved away before any child born to her stepmother would even be old enough for the schoolroom. And she had a houseful—two houses, if she counted Winston's family at Pinehurst—of people willing to love her. She didn't much see the need for a stepmother anymore. Of course, Papa was not terribly old—nearing fifty wasn't nearing death—and he was well within his rights to want a wife and a male heir for the Viscount of Eston title.

Bianca could feel Winston's gaze on her, but he remained silent. They'd discussed all of this when she'd received her father's first letter informing her that he was courting. In all the years he'd gone to town for the sitting of Parliament, this was the first he'd participated in all the social events of the London Season. It had taken a full week of conversations with eminently rational Winston for Bianca to come to terms with it. Thankfully, Papa's first letter had arrived on the heels of Winston's own return from town after spending a fortnight there with his parents. She might have combusted from the confusion of feelings without her friend to talk them through. It had been such a shock that she had barely complained about being left behind and missing out on the sights of London—again.

"Did he tell you any more about her?" Winston asked finally.

Bianca shrugged. "Her name is Malorie Franklin. She's seven-and-twenty and remarkably pretty."

"Then why hasn't she married yet? If she's pretty, you would think someone would have taken her off the market after her first Season or two."

"He didn't say, but it's probably something about her fortune, isn't it? Papa would never care about that, but others might."

Winston nodded. He studied her for a minute, his brow furrowing. "Bee? What else did he say?"

Bianca sighed, wishing her friend couldn't read her so easily. "Nothing, really, only that he thinks she'll be just what we need to prepare me for my entrance into society." A tremor of nerves rippled through her stomach. With her coming out not expected for another three years, she had planned to go on as she was and only start worrying about pleasing the *ton* when the time got closer. Her father and her new stepmother, however, might have other ideas. Somehow she knew that even if she adored this Malorie Franklin—she'd be Malorie

Snow by then—her life was about to change in uncomfortable ways.

Winston made a noncommittal but supportive noise. Before he could comment, however, Harry appeared at the entrance of their little hideout.

"Time to be riding back, Miss Snow. You promised to devote some of the afternoon to history, remember."

Bee sighed and dragged herself out of the cave with Winston on her heels. Nurse wasn't a strict schoolmistress by any means, but Bianca would much rather spend her days riding and boxing than studying. She liked reading well enough on rainy days, but the May weather was too beautiful to waste.

"I'll bring you a new spell tomorrow," Winston offered.

"A good one?"

"Naturally."

She rewarded him with a bright smile. He grinned. She joined Harry and Diamond at the stump that served as a mounting block. Once she was in the saddle, the other two mounted. She and Harry turned toward home with a final wave to Winston, who rode off in the other direction toward Pinehurst.

Eston Hall was a large, whimsical stone house that had begun existence over a century ago at half the size and had been expanded over the years by throwing out a wing here and a garret there. It sat in the middle of a large park with fields, forest, and a large pond perfect for boating. The Viscounts of Eston had lived there for the last three generations. Their neighbors, the Earls of Rowland, had built Pinehurst even earlier, and while the current earl—Winston's father—jovially teased Bianca's father about settling a little close for comfort, nobody actually minded the proximity. The forest that stretched between the houses gave plenty of privacy, and it had provided endless hours of exploration and amusement for Bianca and Winston, who had been inseparable from the moment they'd been allowed to run loose on the estates. Despite the approach of adulthood, no one had tried to curtail their adventures, as long as Harry rode along to ensure Bee's safety.

\*\*\*

Fortunately, Bianca's black eye had returned to normal by the time her father returned home with his new bride. She didn't ride out to meet Winston on the day they were due to arrive, wanting to stay close to home so that she'd be ready and waiting as soon as the carriage rolled up the drive. She was always eager to see Papa after he'd been gone for three months to London, but there was an extra anticipation and apprehension that had her fidgeting in her seat while a maid pinned up her hair. What would her stepmother see when she looked at her? Bee studied herself in the mirror. Hair so dark it was nearly black and so straight it would barely hold a curl, and dark brown eyes to match. Pale skin that refused to gain a golden glow no matter how much she was out in the sun, but at least it didn't freckle. Pink cheeks and rosy lips completed the picture. Her day dress was dark blue and simple, not the latest style but tidy and neatly pressed. At a glance, no one would guess that she'd sported a purplish-green trophy from a sparring match only a week ago, or that she shirked her lessons as often as she could get away with it, or that she made a game of stealing sweets from the kitchen. Bee smiled at her reflection. This was exactly the first impression she was aiming for.

It was another two hours before the carriage rolled up in front of the house, and Bianca spent the time pacing the drawing room. The book she was supposed to be reading—a tedious biography of Charlemagne—lay untouched on the side table alongside a tepid cup of tea. At the sight of the familiar carriage, she hurried to the entrance hall, where she was joined by Nurse and Mrs. Portman, the housekeeper, and a lineup of servants. Nerves fluttered through Bee's chest as Hawke, the butler, opened the door, and two figures entered the hall. The woman clinging to Papa's arm was tallish and lovely: glossy chestnut curls, primrose cheeks, amber eyes. Her lips were red and full, and she was smiling nervously. Her dress was the color of fresh peaches, and it made her glow in the light from the windows. Bee tried to reconcile this fine lady with her long-held daydream of a mother and couldn't. Somehow the knowledge that her new stepmother was only twelve years her senior hadn't quite settled in until they stood face to face. They were practically of an age to be sisters. So she gaped, speechless, as the last lingering hope she'd unknowingly held of having a real mother and a mother's love winked out of existence.

Then Papa stepped forward and said Bee's name, breaking her from her thoughts, and she ran to him, flinging herself into his arms. He swept her up and spun her around, laughing.

"I missed you, Papa," she said softly, so that only he could hear.

"I missed you, too, my little snowflake." His dark eyes sparkled, and he kissed her cheek. Setting her feet on the floor, he turned to the woman who waited hesitantly a few steps behind. "Bianca, I want you to meet Malorie Snow, Lady

Eston."

Bianca swept her best curtsy and met Malorie's shy smile with one of her own. "Welcome, my lady. We're so glad you're here." It might not be the complete truth, but Bee would try to make it so, for her father's sake. The new viscountess might not be the mother she'd subconsciously hoped for, but she decided she could make do with a sister. She'd never had one of those either, and perhaps she'd like that just as well.

Malorie's smile widened slightly, and she curtsied as well. "I'm delighted to meet you, Bianca. Your father talks about you a great deal."

Bee shot Papa a sidelong glance, hoping he hadn't described all her childhood scrapes. She'd gotten into countless, but those were best not spoken of.

"Only the good things, love," Papa murmured with a wink.

Bee relaxed, until she caught the slight lift of Malorie's eyebrows. She stifled a sigh. Papa's comment would only serve to suggest that there were not so good things to tell as well. There went her positive first impression.

Bianca stepped back as Papa introduced Malorie to Mrs. Portman and the rest of the staff then led her up the stairs to the room adjoining his that had been prepared for her. Once they had left the entrance hall, Bee's shoulders slumped, and she hurried up the back stairs to her own room to change into a riding habit. Winston wouldn't be waiting for her, but she needed a good gallop across the park to clear her head.

# Also by Eliza Prokopovits

Ember and Twine

Jewels and Dragons

The Thunderstone Theft

Regency Magic Faerie Tales
   Her Fae Secret
   The Beast's Magician
   Her Forgotten Sea
   Her Cursed Apple

# About the Author

Eliza Prokopovits (pro-COP-o-vits) is a writer and knitting designer. She is obsessed with books, yarn, and dark chocolate. She lives in Pennsylvania with her husband, two boys, and aging goldendoodle.

www.ingramcontent.com/pod-product-compliance
Lightning Source LLC
LaVergne TN
LVHW021812060526
838201LV00058B/3341